"Good to see you after all these years. How have you been?"

"Are you out of your mind?" Colleen asked, her blue eyes molten.

Eric sighed. "Listen. Join me for lunch. We can discuss this like reasonable professionals."

She blinked in surprise. "You…you're asking me to lunch?"

"Why wouldn't I? We used to be friends." He imbued the last word with a meaning only she'd understand.

Her face pinkened. "Those days are long over."

His brain flooded with memories of a different Colleen. A night he absolutely had to put out of his mind during the case. Sleeping with Colleen had been one hell of a beautiful mistake, one he'd never forgotten.…

Would never forget.

Despite the fact that she was back in his life, he aimed to keep everything strictly professional. When it came to Colleen Delaney, that was his only choice.

Dear Reader,

Sometimes destiny is right in front of us, within reach, but we're too afraid to take hold of it. Because of the past, because of fear, because of obstacles we've created in our minds, we don't take the one chance that could make life perfect.

Colleen had her chance years ago with Eric, law school colleague and the only man who ever made forever seem possible. But her fear-filled past drove them apart, until they wound up on opposite sides of the same lawsuit.

Eric would've spun the world for Colleen Delaney, but she broke his heart. He's none too pleased to face her across the courtroom, but he quickly realizes he's never stopped loving her. If only he can convince Colleen he's worth the risk.

I hope Colleen and Eric's reunion reminds you that destiny is right there waiting for you to reach out.

Warmly,

Lynda Sandoval

HER FAVORITE
HOLIDAY GIFT

LYNDA SANDOVAL

Silhouette®

SPECIAL EDITION®

Published by Silhouette Books

America's Publisher of Contemporary Romance

Special thanks and acknowledgment to Lynda Sandoval for her contribution to the BACK IN BUSINESS miniseries.

 SILHOUETTE BOOKS

ISBN-13: 978-0-373-24934-3
ISBN-10:   0-373-24934-9

HER FAVORITE HOLIDAY GIFT

Visit Silhouette Books at www.eHarlequin.com

Printed in U.S.A.

Books by Lynda Sandoval

Silhouette Special Edition

And Then There Were Three #1605
One Perfect Man #1620
*The Other Sister #1851
*Déjà You #1866
**You, and No Other* #1877
†*Her Favorite Holiday Gift* #1934

*Return to Troublesome Gulch
†Back in Business

LYNDA SANDOVAL

is a former police officer who exchanged the excitement of that career for blissfully isolated days creating stories she hopes readers will love. Though she's also worked as a youth mental health and runaway crisis counselor, a television extra, a trade-show art salesperson, a European tour guide and a bookkeeper for an exotic bird and reptile company—among other weird jobs—Lynda's favorite career, by far, is writing books. In addition to romance, Lynda writes women's fiction and young adult novels, and in her spare time, she loves to travel, quilt, bid on eBay, hike, read and spend time with her dog. Lynda also works part-time as an emergency fire/medical dispatcher for the fire department. Readers are invited to visit Lynda on the Web at www.LyndaLynda.com, or to send mail with a SASE for reply to Lynda Sandoval c/o Harlequin Books, 233 Broadway, Suite 1001, New York, NY 10279.

To
Susan Litman, for graciously inviting me
to join the project, and Charles Griemsman,
just for being awesomely you.

Chapter One

Colleen Delaney strode from the executive conference room, shoulders back and head held high… barely. She'd gone a full ten rounds in the ring of office politics and taken her fair share of cheap blows. But in the end, she'd prevailed. The Ned Jones case was all hers.

She should feel triumphant. Exhilarated. Vindicated.

Instead, anger rolled through her veins like spilled mercury, fluid and shining and toxic. The sting of unshed tears burned her eyes and the mere notion of letting them fall deepened her anger. Showing weakness within the palatial walls of McTierney, Wenzel, Scott and Framus?

Not an option.

Not for her.

Not *ever.*

After all these years of grinding through the grunt cases, winning the unwinnables, never uttering a complaint, she'd still had to beg the partners for a boon assignment that should've been hers without question. Unbelievable. She'd devoted her entire law career to this firm, had more than earned their respect—or should've, considering her impeccable track record in the courtroom, her professionalism, her team attitude. The partners should've acknowledged all that and rewarded her for it with the Jones case—*minus* the battle. Because she deserved it, plain and simple. But there was that one small detail....

She was female.

Her jaw tightened.

It wasn't exactly a secret that women weren't welcome in this boys' club, not even when the woman in question kicked the boys' butts all over Chicago's legal system and proved herself more than worthy.

Repeatedly.

McTierney, Wenzel, Scott and Framus, Attorneys-at-Law, had a long history of pressing female lawyers against that glass ceiling until they couldn't breathe anymore. Until they lost their fight. Until they simply…left. Ironically, it was the main reason Colleen had sought out this firm in the first place, which sometimes made her wonder about her sanity. But that infamous glass ceiling lured her as the penultimate challenge. She wanted to punch her fist straight through it in honor of all the excellent female attorneys who'd come and gone, who'd been treated like dirt, who'd given up.

Colleen Delaney didn't give up.

She *would* be the one who busted through to a full partner position if it killed her. The boys could smell her single-minded ambition like prey scenting a hungry lioness on the hunt. It only made them scramble even harder to prevent her from succeeding. Maybe that was her problem. She was too good at her job, too unwilling to be placed into some societal box, too much of a fighter. Yeah? Well, too bad. The old boys could try to keep Lioness Delaney in her place all they wanted. It wouldn't work.

What if you get married?

What if you decide to have babies?

What if you put the firm at a disadvantage because of your damn biological clock?

A new wave of fury crested and broke over her as she recalled the numerous times she'd heard carefully phrased versions of those inconceivable questions while being told some pimple-faced male junior attorney had leapfrogged her for a promotion that should've been hers, for a career-making case that should've landed on her desk. The partners couldn't state outright that she wasn't getting ahead because she was female, of course. But somehow they always managed to drive the point home without crossing any discriminatory lines.

Her conservative Prada pumps echoed like combat boots on the stark marble hallway that led to the cramped, windowless office where she planned to spend as many hours as it took to win this all-important case. Because one thing was certain:

They could give her the worst office in the entire building.

They could downplay her talents and use her reproductive system or the fact that she had the occasional pedicure as an excuse for holding her back.

They could ignore her achievements and treat her like a junior law clerk.

But if she succeeded in winning Ned Jones versus Taka-Hanson, aka Working Man versus The Corporate Monster? No way in hell could Mick McTierney, Richard Wenzel, Harrison Scott or Bill Framus justify not making her partner, and they damn well knew it. This time, she held the reins.

Safely behind the locked door of her claustrophobic cube of an office, she chucked the case files into a messy manila fan on her marred desktop, sank into her chair, rested her forehead in her uncharacteristically shaky hands.

Deep breaths. Calm. Cool.

Regardless of what it took, she'd end up on top this time. Screw the glass ceiling. This case was her golden opportunity to shatter it to hell, once and for all. She'd show them. At this point in her career, she had no choice. She didn't want to start over when she was this close to making partner, making *history* in the firm.

And—sad but true—she'd rather die than end up with a life like her mother's, molding herself into the perfect little wife when the right man—or any willing man—came along. Colleen loved her mother, but she didn't respect her. Couldn't. Sure, she felt guilty about that, but what could she do? The main thing Colleen had learned growing up with her mother's example? She'd rather be hated but respected than loved and pitied.

She didn't need love to thrive.

She needed success.

Autonomy.

So there it was. She would win this case, damn it, and nab the partner position she should've had years ago. And, now that her goal was in sight, nothing, absolutely *nothing* on earth, could throw her off course.

Eric Nelson was staring slack-jawed with disbelief at the paper he held when the door to his temporary work space—a rarely used conference room at Taka-Hanson headquarters—opened. He glanced up to see his old friend Jack Hanson shoulder halfway past the doorjamb and pause.

"Am I interrupting?" Jack gripped the edge of the door. "I knocked, but—"

Eric shuffled the papers aside and shook off his preoccupation. "Not at all. What's up?"

"Wanted to run something by you." Jack crossed the room and sprawled in the chair on the opposite side of the expansive table. He pulled his chin back and studied Eric for a good long stretch. "You look like you've just seen a ghost, pal. Everything okay?"

No. Everything was the opposite of okay. Eric glanced out the window at the gray Chicago skyline. Snow had begun to fall in fat, wet flakes.

Perfect backdrop for his mood.

He hadn't hesitated when Jack asked him to represent Taka-Hanson for this trumped-up wrongful termination case. The two of them went back to their law-school years, and Eric never said no to a friend in need. The high-profile status of the case didn't hurt either. He relished the challenge.

Or, he'd thought so until he'd read the name of the counsel for the plaintiff. Turning back from the window, Eric shook his head, aware he'd been lost in his own thoughts. "Yeah, I'm… Actually, let me ask you something." He shoved his fingers through his already uncooperative hair, blew out a breath. He couldn't bluff Jack Hanson. Did he really want to? "You remember much about law school?"

A wistfulness passed over Jack's expression like swift-moving cloud shadow. Eric knew Jack still missed practicing law, though working for the family business had been the right move after the Hanson patriarch had passed away a few years ago. Losing Jack had been a blow to the law firm, though. One they still felt.

"Every minute of it," Jack said. "Best years of my life, until I met my lovely wife, that is. Why?"

Eric grimaced. "The name Colleen Delaney ring a bell?"

Jack barked a short laugh and interlaced his fingers behind his head. "Your three-year headache?"

"Migraine," Eric said, but it wasn't the entire

truth. She was also the woman who'd stolen his heart, then crushed it. But he'd ignore that aspect of the problem. "That woman was a pain in my—"

"Hot, though," Jack pointed out, aiming a finger Eric's way. "You have to admit that. And you did start out as friends, if memory serves."

Eric shrugged, not about to touch on the topic of Colleen Delaney's "hotness," or what could've been a long-lasting friendship…maybe more…if things hadn't spiraled horribly out of control. "Not for long."

"What happened with that? You never told me."

And he never would. *I fell for her and she unceremoniously dumped me?* Uh, no. That wasn't an admission one guy made to another. "Our personalities didn't mesh," he said instead. "Butting heads with an obstinate woman isn't my idea of a good time." Making love to Colleen by the glow of the streetlight streaming into her apartment window? *That* had been a good time. Better, actually. It had been an emotional epiphany—or so he'd thought.

Jack nodded slowly. "You two did fight like an old married couple. You know, I always suspected there was something between the pair of you."

Eric's ears flamed. He tried to forget that magical night. One of their typical beer-infused legal debates had escalated into something more. So much more. Something amazing—until it all crumbled.

Talk about a colossal mistake.

After one unforgettable night spent in her bed, her personality had done a complete one-eighty. Before that, they'd debated in a friendly way, hung out, studied together and shared a mutual, sizzling attraction. Afterward, her steel walls had slammed down, leaving him strictly on the outside and without a key.

Clearly, he'd been a one-off. If only he'd known that before his heart had gotten involved. Oh, well. Once the sting of the dismissal eased, he'd realized it was for the best. Opposites may attract, but he and Colleen were more like water and electricity than yin and yang. Their kind of opposite was never good. At least, that's what he told himself. "An old married couple who despised each other and never should've gotten hitched in the first place," he said.

"Indeed." Jack cocked his head to one side. "But why the blast from the past?"

"Seems the past is going to explode into the present." He spun the paper he'd been reading around to face Jack. "Delaney's representing Ned Jones."

"You've got to be—" Jack leaned forward and scanned the paper, a slow grin spreading on his face. "I thought that old tight-ass Framus was at the helm?"

"So did I, but she works for the guy. Who knows what happened there."

Jack chuckled. "What are the odds? That's fantastic."

"Fantastic?" Eric spread his arms wide. "The woman hates me. She made every day of law school a living hell. I was never so happy to bid someone a permanent farewell," he said, unsure whether he was trying to convince Jack or himself. Colleen had always been headstrong. But after they'd spent the night tangled up in each other, Colleen Delaney, aka She Who Must Be Right, started to remind him way too much of his loud, competitive family. Almost as if she wanted him to think of her that way. Granted, she was physically beautiful, and he'd always felt a pull toward her. But her penchant for getting in your face and refusing to back down until she could claim victory dimmed her outward attributes and left him cold. He got his share of that sort of stress every time he had dinner at his parents'.

While he could admire her tenacious drive to succeed, he didn't approve of her no-holds-barred tactics. Never had. It wasn't his style and he didn't like to be around people who played the game that way. Despite the fact they both practiced law in Chicago, he'd managed to steer clear of her for years. To face her on opposite sides of a high-profile case *now?* Hell on earth. "I can't believe she popped up. Couldn't be a worse time."

"Like I said," Jack repeated, "what are the odds?"

"It's a nightmare I don't need, Jack. I don't think you understand the problems she's going to cause with the case, simply because I'm on the other side."

Jack let his hands drop to his lap as he studied Eric, a line of worry bisecting his brows. "You want out?"

"Hell, no. That's not what I'm saying."

"Thank God."

Eric frowned. "I wouldn't let you down like that. I'm deep into research and I think I'm onto something big. I've got an angle on this thing."

"Care to share?"

Eric preferred to have all his facts checked and double-checked before sharing theories with a client. Even when that client happened to be a friend. "Let me follow a few more trails. I'll give you a full report once I'm sure I've covered everything pertinent. We're in good shape, though. Stand down all the worriers."

Jack gave a quick nod. "Excellent. As for the Colleen Delaney curveball, you have my sympathy. All I can say is, everything happens for a reason."

Right. Eric wasn't so sure about that. There was no reason beyond karmic cruelty why fate would throw the two of them together again. "Enough of your philosophical rhetoric. I'll handle Delaney. You wanted to run something by me?"

"Yeah. I need your opinion." Jack rubbed the side of his hand against his jawline. "We're bringing Robby Axelrod back from Tokyo to head up the latest hotel project here in Chicago. Any thoughts on how that decision might impact the case?"

Eric sat back, tapping his Mont Blanc pen on the stack of paper in front of him as he methodically puzzled through the myriad of possible ramifications. Ned Jones had filed a wrongful termination suit after having been fired from Taka-Hanson. He'd been about to blow the whistle on Axelrod's—and by extension, Taka-Hanson's—alleged shady construction practices. He claimed they cut corners to save money, skimped on safety, among a litany of other complaints, all at the direction of Robby Axelrod on behalf of the company.

Frankly, Eric thought Jones was full of it. Gut feeling. The guy reeked of disgruntled employee sniffing for a payout. Taka-Hanson needed to present a united front and hide nothing. Hence, bringing Axelrod back served their purpose. "It's a good idea," he said, finally. "Show the world Taka-Hanson backs Axelrod one hundred percent."

Jack's alert posture softened. "I hoped you'd say that. I feel the same way, but you're the boss on this one."

"Giving the man the reins on a massive new hotel

project is a genius strategy, actually. Wish I'd thought of it." Colleen Delaney wouldn't agree with the decision, but he didn't much care. "It reinforces our position that Ned Jones has a self-serving, ulterior motive unrelated to the company's business practices."

"Excellent." Jack stood. "I'll let you get back to it then. I know you've got other cases besides ours." He headed for the door but turned back, one hand on the brushed-metal handle. "Not that you asked for my advice, but as far as this thing with Colleen Delaney? Deal with it just like you did in law school, pal."

Eric snorted. "What—argue with her incessantly, then drink beer with my friends and complain?"

Jack grinned. "That's one option. Before that route, though, try killing her with calmness. So to speak. No actual killing, of course."

Eric cocked his head in question.

"Don't you remember how that used to go down?"

"Guess I've blocked it out." He'd blocked a lot about Colleen out because thinking of it, of her, of what could've been hurt too much.

"Delaney's fueled by a fight," Jack said. "Your Zen attitude? That's her kryptonite. She never knew what to pull out of her arsenal when you went the chill route."

Eric hadn't held on to those particular memories, but come to think of it, true enough. Calmness had always doused the fire of Colleen's argumentative nature. It was as if she didn't know how to handle someone who wouldn't rise to her bait, which worked out great for him. He had no desire for the constant clashing. Lucky for him, he'd had years of practicing law his way—balanced, level, calm. Years of being away from the woman who got under his skin, in more ways than one, and challenged that. Years to forget.

"I suppose it's worth a try."

"Definitely. In fact, go all out and blindside her."

"Meaning?"

"Rekindle the old friendship."

Danger zone. He'd handle her with calmness this time, just as Jack suggested, though he wasn't so sure about befriending her. The rest, though, it could work.

Hopefully.

If not, he'd do his best to ignore her, suffer through the case, then move on with his life once he'd cleared Axelrod and Taka-Hanson, which he had no doubt he could. He hiked his chin toward Jack. "Thanks. Good stuff. I'll take it under advisement."

Jack smiled, smacking his palm on the door a couple times. "If it doesn't work, you know I'm always available for that beer."

Chapter Two

Eric cut a quick path out of the courthouse building. The hearing had gone well enough, which was to say, he hadn't had to speak directly to Colleen. At this point, that constituted a victory.

The moment he'd seen her, his resolve collapsed, telling him without a doubt that he wasn't over her. She'd matured from a hot law student into a fiercely sexy woman. And, despite what she might think, her conservative, man-tailored blue suit and precision-cut, swingy black hair couldn't quite hide her assets.

The broken-glass personality, though? Still as sharp.

When she'd made a motion to bar Robby Axelrod from working on the Taka Hotel project, Eric felt the fury radiate from her like snapped electrical wires. When the judge had denied her request, those wires sparked and exploded in his direction. No chance of putting the calm, friendly approach into play today. Clearly she needed time to cool off. Delaney the Debate Diva was not at all happy about that first loss, the first of many in this case if Eric's research panned out. He had no desire to face her wrath today.

He'd almost made a safe escape when he heard:

"Nelson! Hang on. I need to talk to you."

The click-clack of her determined, angry footsteps approaching brought him to a reluctant stop. He swore under his breath, then remembered Jack's words of wisdom and turned to face her. Calm, cool, confident. Cordial. At least on the outside. He wished Jack had given her the same advice.

She stormed up, chin raised for a fight.

"Colleen," he said in a mild tone, trying not to notice her smooth, touchable skin. Trying desperately not to inhale her signature powdery scent. "Good to see you after all these years. How have you been?"

"Are you out of your mind?" she asked, her blue eyes molten.

Deep breath in, slow release. Apparently being

susceptible to nostalgia wasn't one of her faults. "Nice greeting."

She flicked away his attempts at semipolite conversation as if his words were a mosquito swarm. So much for Jack's plan. "Make your clients take Axelrod off the new hotel project until this case is settled. I mean it."

Oh, she meant it. Good to know. "I'm not talking to you about this here, Colleen. Not when you're tossing off demands without so much as a hello."

He turned and casually walked away.

After a stunned moment, she followed.

"How can you defend those corporate monsters, Eric? That's not your style."

"You know nothing about my style. We haven't spoken in almost a decade."

"Do you have any idea how many lives are potentially at stake thanks to their shoddy construction?"

"Yep." A beat passed. "Exactly…none."

"None?"

Her hand closed around his forearm, a tiny viselike grip of self-righteousness. Resisting the urge to yank away, ignoring the tingles a simple touch sent through his body, he stilled. Stared down at her hand on his arm in relaxed silence until she got the hint and pulled back.

As he looked into her zealous, heart-shaped face,

a pang of compassion struck him for how clueless she seemed to be. She had a pit-bull grip on a fight she would lose, and she didn't seem to have a clue about her client or the big picture. Hard to believe she'd let her lack of research into the case show through her porcupine quills of ire, but as far as he knew, she'd only recently been assigned to it. Maybe she hadn't had adequate time to delve in. Still. No excuse. She needed to do her research and find out what she was dealing with.

Harsh, Nelson.

Eric's overactive conscience kicked in, his emotional pull toward this woman. He didn't want to embarrass her; he simply wanted to exonerate his clients. Sharing what he'd dug up about a possible connection between her client and his client's key rival before she humiliated herself in front of the entire Chicago legal community felt like the right move. He wasn't violating privilege; Jack Hanson didn't even know Drake Thatcher might be involved yet. Contrary to the reputation of most attorneys, he wasn't about putting on the best show in the courtroom. He was about truth and balance and justice.

Fairness.

That meant bringing Colleen up to speed, like it or not. He sighed. "Listen. Join me for lunch. We can discuss this like reasonable professionals."

She blinked in surprise. "You…you're asking me to lunch? Are you crazy?"

He tapped the face of his watch. "Strangely, no. Lunch is what people do around this time of day. It's one of the three widely recognized meals."

"But—"

"Colleen," he said, weary of knocking heads already, "I've been in court all morning. I've got a full slate of work this afternoon. I'm hungry. Is that so hard for you to understand?"

She crossed her arms over her torso. "No. What's hard to understand is why you'd invite me."

"Why wouldn't I? Years ago, we used to be friends." He imbued the last word with a meaning only she'd understand.

Her face pinkened. "Years ago, like you said. Those days are long over."

So she wanted to play it that way. "Look, as much as you hate the fact, I *do* know you. Either I invite you, or I miss lunch altogether because you'll keep me standing here in the hallway arguing ridiculous points of law. I'd like to avoid that if at all possible." He held up his free hand. "Nothing more than that."

She studied him, seeming to search for an ulterior motive. Typical Colleen. After a moment, she tossed her sleek black hair and tried for casual. She didn't quite pull it off. "Fine. Where do you want to go?"

"Let's just hit The Chambers. It's close and easy."

"I'll meet you there."

"We can ride togeth—"

"I said I'll meet you there."

Eric watched her stalk off, shoulders back, spine stiff. Astonishing how she managed to walk so straight with that monumental chip weighing down her shoulder. It had to be one hell of a heavy burden after all these years.

Not his problem.

He shook his head and started toward the parking lot, his brain reluctantly flooded with memories of a different Colleen. Sure, there'd been only one night in their history that the chip had fallen off her shoulder...a night he absolutely had to put out of his mind during this case. Sleeping with Colleen had been one hell of a beautiful mistake, one they'd never spoken about again, despite his repeated attempts shortly thereafter. Initially, he'd been bewildered by her ice-cold attitude, but she wouldn't discuss it. Eventually, he just wrote the woman off as a loose cannon, and his life had been more pleasant since that decision.

That's what he told himself at least.

But he'd never forgotten....

Would never forget.

Couldn't.

Despite the fact she was back in his life, he aimed

to keep everything strictly professional. Sadly, when it came to Colleen Delaney, that was the only choice she'd given him.

Of all the attorneys in Chicago, why Eric Nelson? Stupid Murphy's Law.

Colleen sat in her Audi A6 for several minutes trying to still her nerves, regain her composure. If *any* guy could break her resolve to stay smart, sane and selectively celibate, that guy was Eric. One look at him in that courtroom—broad-shouldered and confident in his charcoal-gray suit, dark blond hair sexily uncooperative as usual—and Colossal Mistake Night flooded back into her body with a vengeance. The sex had been as explosive and exciting as their debates. It had nearly knocked her off her goal path. Or…it could've, had she not freaked out and gone completely cold on the guy, purely by necessity. The whole thing had shaken her to the core, and she hadn't known any other way to handle it.

She'd run scared then, and she'd run scared today.

Thank goodness, Eric had given up the pursuit both times. And while their estrangement hurt, it also bolstered her resolve to be as diametrically opposed as possible to her mother's opinion of what womanhood entailed. That meant no marriage. Possibly no man, which was fine.

Fine, fine, fine.

God, he'd looked fine. She let her eyes drift closed.

He'd been a good-looking guy in law school, but he'd matured into an incredible man with incredible presence. He filled up the space around him, claimed it, sucked the air from the lungs of those nearby. And with a calmness that both drew her in and infuriated her. He still made her tummy flop and her heart flutter, still made her want to argue.

Still made her want to get naked and let everything go.

What a mess.

Colleen smacked the heel of her hand against the leather steering wheel. Unsure what else to do, she fished her cell phone out of her purse and sent a text message to her best friend, Megan, a massage therapist. Megs always talked her down from the various ledges of her life when no one else could. Not that she gave anyone else the chance, but still. Megs was centered, nonjudgmental, soothing. Real.

A lot like Eric Nelson, come to think of it.

No. No. No.

Colleen couldn't risk viewing him that way. It only made things worse.

She just needed to speak with Megan, who knew everything about her and, shockingly, loved her anyway. Go figure. Megan was her safety zone, the one person she could tell absolutely anything. On the other hand, she didn't plan to tell Eric Nelson anything about herself or her life. Ever. She'd gotten too close to that flame once before, and the burn still licked up inside her in moments of weakness.

She quickly typed:

Opposing counsel? Eric Nelson. From law school. THE GUY. Kill me now.

She hit Send and waited. Moments later, her phone rang.

"Hi, sweetie," Megan said, in her just-finished-yoga-and-meditation voice. "You okay?"

Colleen bit her lip and blinked into the cold, wintery brightness. Dirty snow from the last storm clung to the curbs, but the sky gleamed a bright whitish gray. "I don't know. I just… Why him? Of all people? This case is so important, Megs. I can't let our past get in the way of winning."

Megan laughed softly. "Do you ever let anything get in the way of winning?"

Colleen cracked a reluctant smile. "Good point. But it's Eric."

"Yes, it is," Megan said softly.

"And we're meeting for lunch. Now. Ostensibly to discuss the case."

"Let it go. It's just lunch with another professional."

Colleen huffed. "Yeah, a professional I let my guard down with. And had wild jungle sex with." *Life-altering, crushingly intimate, dangerous jungle sex.* "Oh, God," she groaned, squeezing her forehead with her free hand. Heat and something more visceral swirled through her body. An ache. A primal yearning. "I thought I could handle this, but then I saw him and—"

"You can handle it, sweetie. It was a one-night stand back in school. It happens."

"Not to me."

"Well, it did," Megan said, as if it were no biggie. "And nothing ever came of it, so release it."

"You make it sound so simple."

"It can be. You're an amazing attorney, Colleen, and you're going to win this case. Take some deep breaths—you remember the breathing techniques I taught you?"

Oops, busted. "Yes. Definitely." *Too enthusiastic.*

"Are you practicing them daily?"

She considered fibbing. Why bother; Megan would know. "Not exactly…daily."

"Ever?"

"Well, I do *breathe* every day, if that counts."

Megan laughed. "Not the same. How far do you have to drive to the lunch spot?"

"About a mile."

"Okay, the whole way there, breathe deeply and slowly, drawing air clear to the bottom of your lungs. Center yourself. Then go have lunch, focus on the case that's going to make your career, and forget about one meaningless night of sex."

That was the problem. As much as Colleen tried to claim differently, it hadn't been meaningless. It had been beautiful and innocent and *right*. She still remembered the tears trickling from her eyes down the sides of her face to her ears after her first climax. Not because it had been bad, but because Eric made her feel safe in a way no one ever had before. Colleen's belly tightened at the memory. "One night of mind-blowing sex," she said, trying to focus on the physical rather than the emotional.

"Not so easy to forget then, huh?"

She bit her lip, feeling unsure. Unsure and hating herself for it. That was so her mother's style. He was just a man. A man who hated her—she'd made sure of that after the fact. "I have to."

"Then you will."

Colleen's throat closed. She wished she could be more like Megan, but they were cut from different bolts of cloth. She'd accepted that long ago. "Why do you believe in me more than I believe in myself?"

"That's what best friends do. Now, breathe. And call me tonight and tell me all about it."

"Okay."

"And come in for a massage soon."

"I will."

"So…how does he look?"

"Megan! I can't believe you'd ask me that in my time of stress," Colleen said, but she couldn't help laughing.

"Hey, you can't blame me. He's sort of legendary in the life and times of Colleen Delaney."

"It was one *night*." *Keep telling yourself that.*

"Yeah. I know. Of *mind-blowing jungle sex.* You don't hear that phrase every day. So? How does the man look?"

A pause ensued.

"Amazing," Colleen said ruefully, wishing he was paunchy and balding, with a big gin blossom nose, like the partners at her firm. That would make it so much easier not to feel. She couldn't risk feeling. "He looks better than he did during school. Which totally sucks, I might add."

"Well, don't think about it. Try not to look at him."

"Right. Helpful. Should I blur my eyes?"

Megan laughed softly again. "It's all going to be fine in the end."

"How do you know?"

"I just do. Now, go to lunch and do your thing." A smooch sound carried over the line.

"What's my thing, though? Help!"

Megan cleared her throat. "You do realize this is what you've always done, right?"

"Huh?"

"Freak out about Eric Nelson, then call me?"

"I'm not freaking out, Megs. Freaking out is what teenagers do. I'm just—"

"Go to lunch," Megan said, laughing.

For the life of her, Colleen couldn't find a single thing funny with this nightmare....

Chapter Three

"You do realize this is what you've always done, right?"

"Huh?"

Jack laughed as though he hadn't a care. "Freak out about Colleen Delaney, then call me."

Eric shook his head as he navigated a turn on the icy Chicago streets. "I'm not freaking out, Jack. Freaking out is what fifteen-year-old boys do at the first glimpse of bikini-clad cleavage on the Navy Pier every spring."

"Case? Rested."

"The woman gets under my skin, that's all."

"Interesting," Jack mused.

"Not that kind of under my skin," Eric lied, pulling into an empty curbside spot near The Chambers, a popular eatery with legal types and others who worked at the courthouse. He cut his engine. "I spoke to her for all of five minutes and I'm sure my blood pressure skyrocketed." He wouldn't tell his old friend exactly why. "She's argumentative. Prickly. Annoying."

"Which you hate." Jack's statement didn't sound convincing.

"As a matter of fact, I do."

"Is she still totally hot?" Jack asked, a smile threaded through his words.

Eric closed his eyes for a moment. Strength. He needed strength and lots of it. Yes, Colleen Delaney had never been hotter, but that didn't help the situation. "Never mind. I need to go. The tables get snatched up this time of day."

"You and Colleen have a nice lunch," Jack drawled. "Give her a kiss from me."

"I'm sure she'd appreciate hearing that from the man her client's suing," Eric said in a droll tone, before hanging up, more exasperated than when he'd called his old pal. Jack seemed determined to paint his relationship with Colleen in rosy tones, and Eric couldn't put himself into that position again. Official verdict: love and marriage had warped Hanson's brain. That's the only explanation Eric could come up with.

A welcoming warmth enveloped him as he entered The Chambers. He inhaled the familiar aromas of coffee and grilled burgers and hot apple pie, and his mouth watered. Midday service was in full, bustling swing. He brushed snowflakes from the shoulders of his wool overcoat, stamped his feet on the mat.

"Just one?" asked the hostess, who'd swirled up in mid-busy, her movements compact and efficient. "Wanna sit at the counter?"

He smiled. "Actually, I'm meeting someone. Do you have a table? Preferably someplace quiet."

"We don't get much quiet at lunchtime as you know, but…" The petite blonde tapped her bottom lip with her index finger and scanned the dining room, which was filled with the tink-tink of fork against plate and a healthy serving of boisterous legal debate punctuated by laughter and movement. Stark contrast to the snow-quieted city outside the large windows. Eric was convinced that snow was God's way of telling the human race to shut up and simply be.

A group of lawyers Eric vaguely recognized but couldn't name stood up from a table in the back corner and began donning overcoats, gloves and wool scarves. The hostess turned back, her thumb aimed over her shoulder at the group of men. "I can have that table bussed for you if you don't mind waiting a couple of minutes."

"That's fine. She hasn't arrived yet anyway."

"Great." The hostess gave him a pert grin. "It'll be clean and ready when your girlfriend gets here."

Eric opened his mouth to correct the young woman's misconception—why, he didn't know— but she'd left as quickly and competently as she'd arrived.

Had the whole world gone soft on him?

Could a man and a woman *not* share a business meal without people thinking it was something more?

Then again, did it matter?

The ding of the entry bell announced another lunchtime arrival. Eric glanced over his shoulder just as the swoosh of the door brought in a gust of cold along with Colleen, her alabaster cheeks cotton-candy pink from the weather, raven hair flecked with fat, white snowflakes.

Their eyes met.

His heart stuttered.

She dropped her gaze.

He took a slow breath and resisted the urge to

wick away the snowflake that had landed, shimmering and perfect, on her left cheekbone. He could make out the unique design of it, and against the backdrop of Colleen's face, the effect staggered him. Swallowing past this unexpected, unwanted, unnerving visceral pull toward her, he said, "They're cleaning a table."

"Fine," she said, unknotting a cornflower-blue cashmere scarf that matched her eyes and shrugging out of her tailored gray tweed coat. As she stuffed the scarf inside one coat sleeve, she added, "Parking's a real joy around here," in a wry tone.

"Just like always," Eric said, utterly distracted by the snowflake melting on her perfect cheek. "Did you have to walk far?"

Her gaze, wary as ever, met his for one quick moment before darting away. She draped her coat over one arm and shrugged her handbag higher on her shoulder. "It wasn't a problem." Fully melted, the former snowflake trickled down her cheek like a teardrop. She brushed the moisture away, unaware of his fixation on it. "How about you?"

"What?" He pulled himself back into the conversation, if you could label their lame, superficial exchange as such. "Oh. No. I'm right out front."

"Still have that legendary Nelson parking karma then."

"Something like that," he said, surprised that she'd remembered. For some reason, whenever he envisioned the perfect parking spot, it always appeared for him. It'd been that way since he'd gotten his license at sixteen, and a source of great envy and many conversations among his law-school classmates years ago.

But whatever. This small talk was the worst.

He'd never been a pro at it, and never with a woman like Colleen, who threw him so totally off-kilter. He wanted to ask what happened between them. Wanted to know if their single night together had been as life-affirming for her.

He wanted to touch her.

None of that was going to happen, though, and they had to converse. He cleared his throat. "Do you eat here often?" Had he seriously just asked that? He resisted the urge to cringe. That ranked high on the dumbest questions ever asked list. Maybe he was just like those cleavage-obsessed teenage boys at the Navy Pier.

"Not really," she said, seemingly unaware of his discomfort. "I live nearby."

He nodded, unsure what to say about that. He lived nearby, too, but he ate here at least four times a week. Was it a male versus female thing, or was that sexist? He wondered if cooking was a hobby and she preferred to eat at home, or if she packed a lunch. He wondered how she lived her life. He wondered, simply wondered, about Colleen Delaney.

Clearly, she didn't have much to add, and he didn't know where to go in the conversation, now that they'd skipped from point uncomfortable to point awkward. Did he really want to take another leap to point excruciating? They waited, shoulder to shoulder, in pregnant silence until the elfin blonde bopped up and led them to their corner booth.

Safely behind menus on opposite sides of the table, Eric breathed more easily. He glanced up at Colleen. "How's your mother?"

Colleen blinked, as if startled by the intimacy of the question or the fact that he'd give a rip in the first place. Something. "My mother?"

"Yeah. You know, she's that woman who gave birth to you back in the day?"

Colleen ignored his quip. "She's fine. Well, getting better finally."

"Was she ill?" He set his menu aside, knowing he'd order the French Dip, like always. Perusing the menu at The Chambers was purely habit.

Colleen shook her head. "Not sick, really. She had a knee replacement. Injured it trying to surf with her last boyfriend," she added, her tone acidic.

"That's awesome."

"If you say so. I moved her into my place to recover, and now we're apparently permanent room-mates."

"Wow." He thought about any member of his family moving into his serene, lovingly restored greystone Victorian, and one word came to mind—hives. "How's that working out for you?"

Eyebrows raised, Colleen set her menu on the edge of the table as well. "I'm not sure. She drives me crazy half the time, rearranging my kitchen utensils, putting my clean laundry away in spots where I can't find it, nagging me about working too hard." She hiked one shoulder, and the tenor of her voice changed. "The other half, it's nice to have her there, I suppose."

"Welcome to the definition of family."

A moment of silence descended. Colleen tugged at her cuffs, uncrossed and recrossed her legs, cleared her throat. Finally, she asked, "And your family?"

"Pretty much the same as the last time we talked." Which had been…wow…a long time ago. "Mom and Dad still live out in Schaumburg and expect us all there promptly at six for Friday-night dinner, no excuses."

She spared him a half-smirk. "Your least favorite night of the week still?"

He tilted his head to the side. "You remembered."

Ignoring that, she asked, "And your brothers?"

"My youngest brother, Brian, settled down not too far from them. The other three are here in Chicago. Working, one-upping each other at every turn, the annoying norm." He often wondered how he'd grown up to be so different from his ultracompetitive family. They could—and did—debate about everything from gold values to golf to global warming, with the single-minded goal of winning, no matter what. And when he didn't want to debate, which was often? They goaded him. Like rabid dogs.

"Married?"

Eric assumed Colleen wasn't asking about him. "Only Brian. He works with my dad at the store."

"A sporting-goods store, right?"

"Yep." He formed two L shapes with his hands and thumbs, as if framing the sign that had hung on the main drag in Schaumburg since he could remember. "Nelson Sports and Hunting. Still running strong."

"Good for your dad."

He watched Colleen tilt her head to the left, which always meant she was thinking, calculating.

"Now, wait. Isn't Brian pretty young?"

"The 'oops' brother?" Eric nodded. "Yes, twenty-one. And Melody—that's Brian's wife—is only twenty. She works as a receptionist at a small law firm in the city and she runs some idiotic gossip Web site on the side. Typical twenty-year-old." He reconsidered his judgmental comment at the slight shocked widening of Colleen's blue eyes. "I could've phrased that better. The idiotic site will be a good source of income, I guess, when the baby comes. Oh, they're expecting, Brian and Melody. My mother's losing her mind with happiness. A baby. Extended family. New Nelson generation and all that."

"That's…nice."

"Yeah, all I can think of is Brian becoming a father the same year he's legal to drink. Crazy."

"That is…wow." She sat back. "They're young. Are they ready for parenthood?"

"Do they have a choice at this point?"

"True."

The conversation felt so casual, it lulled Eric into a sense of normalcy. "It's good to see you. You look great, Colleen. Really."

Her eyes hardened and the thin line of connection between them snapped like a dried-out rubber band. "We need to talk about the case."

Duly noted. No compliments. She never had been the kind of woman who liked to be admired for her considerable beauty, but come on. It wasn't like a guy didn't notice. He'd known about her pet peeve, of course, but what else did you say when you saw someone for the first time in years? So she looked great. Shoot him for pointing it out.

Just then, the harried waiter approached, plunked two glasses of water on the table. "Sorry for the wait," he said, slightly out of breath. "What can I get for you?"

They placed their orders. Once the waiter had bustled off, Colleen seemed to have regained some of her flash and fire. "Honestly, how can you stand by and let Robby Axelrod work on another Taka-Hanson project?"

Eric took his time. He leaned back, stretching his arm along the back of the brown leather banquette. "How much do you know about Ned Jones?"

"What kind of question is that?" she rasped, color rising to angry spots on her cheeks. "He's my client."

"Right. Aware of that. And how much do you know about him?" The calm thing was getting easier by the moment.

Her lips flattened into a grim line. "I know he was unfairly, unethically terminated because he had dirt on your client."

"If that's all you know, you need to dig deeper."

Her knuckles, wound together on the tabletop,

whitened, and she went deadly still. "Are you honestly sitting here telling me how to do my job?"

He counted to ten silently. Why did everything with Colleen devolve into a fight? He started to remember why they were better apart, but strangely, he didn't want to fall back into that pattern. "I'm trying to do you a favor, from one old friend to another."

"My client—"

"Is not the bad guy," Eric said gently. That snagged her attention. He waited until she'd closed her mouth, an indication she was listening. "At least, I don't think he's the brains behind anything. Gut feeling."

"The man doesn't have the brains to concoct a plot."

Ah, so she did know a bit more about her client than she'd initially claimed. "That's what I'm trying to tell you. I think he's the pawn in a much bigger, uglier game."

Confusion crinkled Colleen's brow. She leaned in. "What exactly are you talking about, Eric?"

Eric wrapped his hands around the warm coffee mug the waiter had unobtrusively set before him as they spoke. "I don't know. I'm not sure yet, but this whole thing stinks. You may simply want to win, which I can understand. But I want to do the right thing."

"Of course."

Eric gut-checked sharing this information, and felt fine with it. He blew out a breath.

"Are you familiar with a real-estate tycoon by the name of Drake Thatcher?"

She spread her arms. "Should I be?"

He huffed. "Yes. You should. He's Taka-Hanson's biggest competitor, dirty as Tony Soprano. He'll do anything to take down my clients." He paused, scrutinizing her. "Up to and including paying your client to toss out false accusations."

Her throat moved in a tight swallow, but she maintained her cool. "You have proof of that?"

"No." He ran his fingers through his hair.

"Then why are you wasting my time with unsubstantiated theories?"

"Because an innocent man shouldn't have his livelihood destroyed for no good reason. Taka-Hanson shouldn't take a major financial blow on the basis of a lie. As ambitious as you are, even you have to agree with that."

He could see her annoyance building in the way the muscles worked in her delicate jawline. Tense silence stretched taut between them, but he held his ground.

She aimed a finger at him. "Listen, Nelson, I've been practicing law as long as you have. This kind of ploy—"

"Here we go," said the waiter, in an oblivious singsong tone. "Be careful now. The plates are hot."

Colleen pinched the bridge of her nose between her fingers while the waiter presented each, but her hard gaze never left Eric's face.

"Can I get you anything else?"

"No. Thank you," Eric replied.

After the waiter had left without so much as an acknowledgment from Colleen, she started to sputter again, but Eric held up his palm. "Look, there's no ploy. I don't operate that way. But don't take my word for it. Research me. Dig up everything you can about the way I practice."

"I will. And I'll prove you wrong about Jones."

"Think about this logically. You're the opposing counsel, Colleen, and aside from that, we don't exactly have an uncheckered past, you and I."

"You always did have a knack for putting things mildly."

"I'm speaking truthfully. If I didn't have respect for you as an old friend, a colleague, and from everything I've read, a damned sharp attorney, I'd keep my theories to myself until I had enough to annihilate you and Ned Jones in the courtroom. Which I would." He paused, letting that sink in. "Lucky for you, that's not how I practice law."

"So you're doing me a favor?"

"No. I'm—" He lowered his chin, measured his words. "I'm not about the show, I'm about the truth, and I think we're missing parts of the truth in this case. You can ignore what I'm telling you and let the cards fall, or you can look into it. I don't care." He took a languid bite of his sandwich and shrugged while he chewed. After swallowing, he added, "But I know you're one step from partner at that firm of yours, though God only knows why you'd want to work with that pack of old-school drones."

Colleen's mouth dropped open, but she quickly closed it. Her reaction told him she thought they were old-school drones, too, which made him wonder why she wanted to build a career there. An imponderable for another day.

"That's not going to happen if you miss something major like, say, an extortion plot in which your client is a player," he said. "I promise you that."

"God, Eric, you sound like you're writing a cheesy legal thriller."

"Maybe so, but I think I'm onto something." He shrugged. "Frankly, I'd love to see you make partner at your firm. Framus would bust a vein."

Whoa, had she almost *smiled* there?

She still hadn't touched her burger. Instead, she stared at him with incredulity overlayed by a film of worry she couldn't quite hide, then huffed out a nonlaugh. "So you're telling me I have no case in order to save my career? How chivalrous of you. Don't take me for an idiot."

Eric didn't react. He didn't engage. He *didn't* want their every interaction to end this way. "I take you for a lot of things, but idiot isn't one of them," he said, even-toned. Suspicion crossed her expression, but he'd just let her wonder about the subtext of his statement. "This one's on you. I've shared what I suspect."

"And what am I supposed to do with it? Take your word? Drop the case on the basis of an unproven theory? I don't think so."

"Colleen," he said smoothly, measuring his words. "Your burger's getting cold. Eat your lunch. Then research me. Research Drake Thatcher and any possible connection he may have to your client. Research Robby Axelrod's clean work record. That's what I'll be doing, and that's what you should do, too. For your own sake."

Chapter Four

Colleen glanced up from her laptop screen when her mom padded into the dark kitchen, yawning.

Moira Delaney stopped short, clapping her hand over her heart. "Lord, you scared me."

"Sorry," Colleen croaked, before clearing her throat.

"Sweet pea, what on earth are you doing up at this hour?"

"I'm working, Mom," Colleen said, her voice hoarse from exhaustion. Tension. "What else?"

"But it's nearly four!" her mom exclaimed, glancing at the wall clock. She pulled a tumbler out of the cabinet and filled it with filtered water from the fridge door. "You need your sleep."

Colleen wanted to disagree, but her eyes felt scrubbed with steel wool, and her limbs ached deep into the bone. She simply hadn't been able to tear herself away from the mother lode of information she'd dug up on Drake Thatcher. Eric had been correct about one thing—Thatcher was dirty, and he had a history of trying to take the Hansons down. The question remained, was her client mixed up in any of it?

If so, she'd be screwed. Utterly screwed.

She needed to talk to Ned, get to the bottom of this fiasco before it blew up in her face, and she was intent on gathering as much background data before she dragged his sorry ass into her office tomorrow morning.

Robby Axelrod came off as squeaky clean.

As did Eric, naturally.

She sat back and rubbed her palms over her face, then slapped her cheeks, hoping for a jolt of alertness so she could draw out a game plan. It didn't come.

Her mom poured a second tumbler of water and set it on the table next to Colleen's computer, then brushed her daughter's hair back with a gentle hand. It had to be exhaustion, because the sweet, motherly touch nearly brought Colleen to tears, and she wasn't usually susceptible to sentiment. Especially not from her mother. Thanks to seeing Eric again, thanks to his typical altruistic gesture of bringing Thatcher to her attention, her deeply buried emotions had risen to the top of her skin like raw sores. Usually, her mother's innuendos that she worked too hard—even something as innocuous as bringing her water or brushing her hair back—would irritate her, perhaps provoke an argument. Right now, she felt too vulnerable to react in her usual mode.

She smiled weakly. "Thanks."

"I know you're working an important case, okay? But go to bed. Whatever it is you think you have to finish will wait a few hours. And you'll be better able to handle it if you're rested."

Colleen nodded, bit her bottom lip. As she powered down her laptop, she asked, "Why are you up?"

"Oh, the knee." Mom tightened her robe around her waifish middle. "Just a little ache."

"Is there anything I can do?"

"Yes." Moira smiled. "You can go to bed. I'll be fine in about half an hour. I'm just going to watch television until the painkiller kicks in."

The mood felt so intimate, so neutral, so unlike their norm, Colleen ventured further into the emotional minefield she usually avoided. "You need to get out more now that your knee's almost healed, Mom. Enjoy the city. Visit a museum."

"Oh, well…"

Colleen closed the top of her computer. "What are your plans for tomorrow?"

"I thought I'd tidy up. Read some." She avoided her daughter's gaze.

"Are you depressed?" Colleen asked, in a soft tone. "The doctors said that can happen after a surgery like the one you had."

Moira Delaney sighed, raked her fingers through her hair, crossed her arms. "Do you want me to move out? Is that it?"

Colleen stood and held her hands up, palms forward. "No. No, Mom. You're welcome to stay here as long as you want. I just want you to…I don't know, enjoy life."

Those cornflower-blue eyes so much like her own pierced Colleen. "Do *you* enjoy life?"

Wow. Hadn't seen that blow coming. It landed right in the sweet spot and made her see stars. "Yes. Of…of course. My work is—"

"Not work," Moira said, flicking her words aside. "You should work to live, not live to work. I'm asking you to tell me the last time you had fun. Frivolous, carefree fun."

The walls of Colleen's penthouse loft swayed

inward, sucking away the oxygen in the room. She took a step back, stared down at the travertine floor. She couldn't get defensive; she'd initiated this mother-daughter bonding chat at her own peril. But the most pathetic part was, she couldn't remember the last time she'd experienced true joy. The carefree, laughing, splashing-in-the-surf kind.

She'd splurged on some bronze Jimmy Choo boots a couple weeks earlier—that had been hedonistically enjoyable. But, if she were completely honest with herself, she'd only indulged in the retail-therapy session because McTierney had totally pissed her off that day at work.

That didn't exactly count as carefree fun.

More like emotional eating, but without the food.

She sighed, glancing across the room at the woman who looked like an older version of herself, but with whom she shared no discernible personality traits. She wished she knew who her father was, what he was like. What made him tick and if she was the same. Her mom was still waiting for an answer, though, and Colleen didn't think she could evade the question. "I can't think. I'm sure I've done something fun. But I'm just too tired."

For some odd reason, Eric Nelson popped into her head. His perpetually disheveled dark blond hair, steady gaze. His broad shoulders. As much as she'd tried to maintain her annoyance during their shared lunch, she had enjoyed being in his company. Being near him had always simultaneously settled and excited her. Her stomach fluttered; she pushed the images away. Maybe she was more like her mother than she wanted to admit. "But I'll make you a deal."

Moira cocked her head. "What's that?"

"I'll do something fun this month if you promise me you'll get out of the house."

"Maybe we can do something fun together out of the house," Moira suggested, her voice tentative.

Colleen pursed her lips, nodded slowly. "Maybe. I'm really busy, but I'll think about it." She didn't miss the slight fall of her mother's hopeful expression. That was problemo number one. Her mother didn't have a life outside this apartment, outside the daughter who resented her, outside a lifelong disappointing search for that ever-elusive man who would take care of her. And even man-hunting had fallen by the wayside of late.

The whole thing was too much for Colleen to think about with her already bleary brain. She couldn't be her mother's *everything*. "I'm hitting the sack. I can't keep my eyes open a moment longer."

"Good girl. I'll keep the television low."

"Thanks. I don't think it'll matter."

Just before she'd exited the shadowed kitchen, her mother called out to her softly.

"Colleen?"

"Yeah, Mom?"

"I love you, pea. Thank you for…taking me in."

A resentful silence stretched when it shouldn't have, and Colleen chastised herself inside. Why was it so damned difficult for her to open up to the woman who'd brought her into this world? A daughter shouldn't struggle to say three simple words to her own mother. She swallowed past a suddenly tight throat and the overwhelming need to escape. "Love you, too," Colleen said in a half-whisper. "Good night."

In the clearer light of day, Colleen decided it would be smarter to confront Ned Jones away from the office. If the partners sniffed out the potential firestorm on the horizon, they'd find a way to cast her as the scapegoat. On top of everything else going haywire in her world at the moment, she didn't need that. She wanted as much of this case as possible under control before she broke the news to anyone at her firm, and she wanted answers.

Unannounced, she drove to Ned's apartment, an unkempt building in one of the city's "emerging neighborhoods," a real-estate euphemism for "seedy." Icy air burned her nostrils as she picked her way over the snow-crusted, cracked pavement, pushed through the propped-open front door, and climbed four flights of creaky stairs to apartment 4B.

Bam! Bam! Bam!

She crossed her arms and waited. He had to be home. From what she'd come to learn about the guy, he didn't do much these days except wait for his payoff from the lawsuit.

"Who is it?" came his muffled voice through the door.

"It's Colleen Delaney, Ned. I need to talk to you."

She waited through a series of dead bolts being thrown before the door squeaked open about four inches, hindered by the safety chain. Ned peered out through the crack.

"It is you," he said, sounding surprised.

As if she'd lie? Or someone else would pretend to be her? She spread her arms wide in lieu of answering.

Ned shut the door, disengaged the chain, then opened it fully. He ran a hand through his messy hair and glanced back at his even messier apartment. "If I'd known you were coming—"

"It's fine," she said. "May I come in?"

"Sure, sure." He moved aside.

Colleen stepped over the threshold and gave the place a cursory once-over. If ever a man had fallen from grace, Ned Jones was that guy. From working as an accountant on a major international hotel construction site to living in a sad little box of an apartment piled with junk. How quickly a life could change in this world.

"What's up?" he asked.

He seemed nervous. She decided to test him. "Drake Thatcher?"

Blood drained from his face like a watercolor left in the rain. "W-what about him?" He gestured her toward the kitchen, scurrying off ahead of her.

His reaction? Red flag. Thatcher was dirty and Ned knew about it, obviously. But she wanted the whole scheme spoken aloud, right here, right now. Once in the kitchen, Ned sat. She loomed above him. Anger reared and bucked inside her, but she fought to tame it. Ripping into the guy might be satisfying, but it wouldn't get her anywhere productive. Instead, she laid out what she'd discovered in her research, and simply asked him to come clean with her. He wouldn't.

She cajoled.

He avoided.

She rationalized.

He hedged.

She begged.

He clammed up.

Finally, out of options and fed up, she unleashed

that wild anger. "Listen to me. You don't have a choice here. This whole thing could very well blow up in our faces. I could be disbarred, you could land in jail. Tell me what the hell is going on, Ned. The truth."

Ned's eyes darted to the chipped linoleum floor, not meeting her gaze. "I'm just not sure I should say anything," he said, in that beat-down, nasally tone that made her want to wrap her hands around his neck. "I have a lot at stake."

"Damn it!" Colleen slammed both palms onto his messy kitchen table, rattling the assortment of dirty dishes piled at the edges like raggedy squatters against a high-rise building. She leaned forward into his face. "*We* have a lot at stake. *We.* I'm your attorney, so I'm irrevocably involved. What part of that do you not understand?"

"I know, but—"

She stopped him, holding up her palm. "Let me put it to you in simple terms. If you continue to lie to me, we're done. If you've worked some stupid deal to make money, we're done. If you blow this case for us because you cannot comprehend the simple concept of attorney-client privilege, *we're done.* No case, no win, no money for you. How much clearer can I be?"

Ned wrung his fingers together, elbows braced

on the table, and bonked the knot of his white-knuckled hands against his forehead, which had begun to perspire.

Colleen's exasperation blew like a mushroom cloud after a bombing. He wasn't just holding out on her, he was toying with her career. She couldn't believe she'd fought for his case, and now it could destroy her. Talk about irony. "I'm trying to help you here, but I can't help you if you're less than honest. Cut the crap and tell me everything. From the beginning, start to finish."

Standoff.

Weak, wintery light struggled in through the small, dirty window, highlighting the crud buildup on the cluttered countertops. Ned Jones not only needed a brain, he needed a housekeeper. And a swift kick in the rear, which she'd gladly provide.

Thin and slump-shouldered, Ned sighed, stared out to the building next door. "What's this going to do to the case?" he asked, in a defeated monotone that told Colleen he was finally ready to spill it all.

"I don't know until you come clean with me," she said, with a sigh, before easing down into the rickety chair and threading her fingers into the front of her hair. "I'll do everything I can to win it. That's my job. But you cannot send me into that courtroom blind. I need to know what I'm up against so I can devise a plan of attack. And I need to know it *now.*"

Time dragged on, marked only by the ticking of the kitchen clock, a cheap plastic number festooned with a ring of garishly painted fruit.

After an eternity, Ned said, "Okay."

Okay? Colleen peered up at her client, half afraid to hear what he might say. Half afraid he'd change his mind. Her stomach knotted. "So?"

He blew out a breath, then swore. "I'm going to need a drink for this, though. Care to join me?"

Never. "No. Thanks."

"Suit yourself." He pushed to his feet then scuffed to his liquor cabinet, extracting a bottle of whiskey and a cloudy, obviously well-used jelly jar.

Colleen watched him pour one, two, three fingers of hooch, and her insides imploded. She squeezed her eyes shut.

God help her.

Eric's preposterous theory had been right. She could feel it. Did he know yet? Did she have an obligation to go to him as he'd done with her? If she did, it was game over. No case, no win, no partnership.

This wasn't going to be good. Not good at all.

Realization hit her like a sledgehammer. She'd made her share of mistakes in life, but this one trumped the entire lot. Every single goal she'd struggled to achieve hung on the bony shoulders of this weak, deceptive, money-grubbing man living in a sad, filthy apartment, drinking whiskey out of a jar at nine in the morning.

Chapter Five

Eric had a full day of work, including meeting Robby Axelrod, fresh off the plane from Tokyo. He was en route to meet with hotel manager Greg Sherman before Greg left for Kyoto; Chicago was merely a pit stop at Taka-Hanson headquarters. But when ninety-year-old Esther Wellington showed up with the glow of hope in her eyes and a recommendation from her grandson—a former client of Eric's—he simply couldn't turn her away.

"We don't know where else to turn, Mr. Nelson." The diminutive woman looked like a fragile fabric doll sitting across from his desk. She wore a fitted wool suit in baby blue with a string of pearls, and the well-earned lines in her crepe-thin face seemed somehow deepened by worry, though he'd only just met her. "I've consulted one law firm who couldn't help us pro bono, and the money—" she shook her head "—it's gone. Time's short, too. My grandson speaks so highly of you, but I know you're busy with clients who can pay."

"Not a problem. I take on pro bono work regularly to feed my soul, not my bank account." He tried to brush his hair away from his face, but most likely it went off in its own direction like normal. He'd never had cooperative hair, not that he cared. "I need to make sure we have a solid case here, that's all."

"If you're unable to represent us, I just don't know…"

Eric smiled at Esther. "Try not to worry. Let me just go over these papers one more time." He buzzed his secretary. Moments later, Jennifer entered his corner office. "Did you need something?"

"Yes. Could you take Mrs. Wellington to get a cup of coffee?" He glanced at the older woman. "Unless you'd prefer tea, of course?"

"At this point, I'd love a gin and tonic," she said.

Eric and Jennifer laughed in surprise, which brought a small, prim smile to Esther's lips.

"However, in lieu of a tipple, tea sounds lovely." She stood and smoothed her skirt. "Thank you very much."

"Come with me, Mrs. Wellington," Jennifer said. "We'll get you all set up in the lounge."

"I'll have Jennifer bring you back just as soon as I've read through everything," Eric added.

After the women left, Eric dug in.

The case seemed straightforward; it happened too often. A small group of elderly folks scraped up enough funds to rehab an old home into a neighborhood senior center. The contractor they hired quoted them one price, did the work, then presented a bill for triple the quote, claiming unexpected costs. None of which he'd brought to their attention during the construction process, of course, which, according to Esther, had seemed to progress without a problem. The group didn't have the funds to pay the exorbitant fees, so he sued. He probably had the whole scheme planned out from the moment he put in his bid.

Folks like Esther didn't need this kind of stress.

Eric's grip tightened on the papers. If you asked him, people who took advantage of the elderly earned themselves a one-way ticket to a special circle of hell. Eric felt like he had a handle on this suit, and he'd go after this guy with guns blazing. But none of that would matter if the case had a fatal flaw. He needed to know why the other law firm declined it. Lucky for him, Esther kept copious notes.

He leafed through until he found her log, written in fine blue willow-branch script. He traced his finger down the page, and a slow smile spread his face.

Well, well, well.

McTierney, Wenzel, Scott and Framus.

Perfect. Everyone knew how that coldhearted, money-driven firm operated. Odds were they hadn't rebuffed Esther due to intrinsic problems with the case. He'd bet his yearly income they'd turned her down because taking on this cause wouldn't pad their already fat wallets.

Scum. Why on earth did Colleen want to work there?

Someday, he'd get her to answer that question.

Representing Esther and the others was the right thing for Eric to do, and busy as he was with the Taka-Hanson situation and the rest of his caseload, he wouldn't hesitate to help the bilked elderly group. Plus…okay, he never claimed to be a saint. He'd admit to a secondary, albeit minor, motive.

Colleen.

He couldn't get her out of his mind. He'd been

searching for a plausible reason to contact her again, to talk to her, to simply be around her, and this provided the perfect vehicle. Looking for background information. Safe. Neutral.

Believable.

Closing the file folder, he buzzed Jennifer again.

She peeked in the door. "Ready for her? She's a doll."

"She is. And I am ready." He smiled. "Thank you."

Moments later, Esther Wellington, tea in hand, slipped through the door, her features luminous with hope. "Have you come to a decision, Mr. Nelson?"

He stood, gesturing toward the chair. "I have. Please, take a seat."

Once they were settled, Eric steepled his fingers. "I think we have a solid case here."

Esther released a whoosh of breath. "Thank goodness."

"I'll be happy to represent you and the others."

Tears shone in Esther's eyes, the teacup rattling on the saucer in her hands. "Oh, bless you. Bless you."

Eric stood and eased the cup and saucer from Esther's grip, placing them on the desk. He offered her a tissue, then sat and waited while she wiped her eyes and composed herself.

With a sniff, she asked, "Where do we start?"

He cleared his throat. "I noticed you consulted with the firm of McTierney, Wenzel, Scott and Framus. Can you tell me which attorney you spoke to and why he decided not to take the case?"

"Oh, *she,* actually. It was the lovely young woman." Esther gazed off in the distance and fiddled with her pearls. "What was her name?"

Eric's heart contracted. "Colleen? Colleen Delaney?"

"Yes! That's her. What a dear."

"Yet, she chose not to take the case?"

"She wanted to," Esther said. "At least, it seemed as such." She leaned in and lowered her tone, as if she and Eric were being watched. "I got the feeling the decision came from over her head, if you know what I mean."

Eric nodded, careful to keep his expression neutral. "Well, Ms. Delaney is a wonderful attorney. I'm sure she did want to help you. But, in her stead, I will do everything in my power to win this case. I'm confident I can."

"You're a true hero, Mr. Nelson."

"No, I'm just a lawyer. And please, call me Eric." He winked. "Mr. Nelson makes me sound like my dad."

Esther tittered behind her blue-veined hand as Eric pondered his run of luck. This pro bono case had fallen into his lap at exactly the right moment. He could put an unethical contractor in his place, help out a wonderful group of older folks, and have a legitimate excuse to get in touch with Colleen. Interesting. As he picked up the phone and dialed, he thought back to Jack's words the day they'd found out Colleen was representing Ned Jones, and shook his head.

Maybe everything *did* happen for a reason.

Colleen pressed the replay button on her cellphone voice mail again—for about the tenth time.

"Hey, Colleen, it's me. Ah, Eric, that is. Nelson. Shoot, you probably knew that," his voice muttered in a rush that made her smile. Every time. "Anyway, I need to speak with you about a case. Not the Jones case, something else. Call me. Anytime, okay? Here are my numbers."

She had his home, cell and office numbers written on a notepad next to her bed, and she had his voice recorded. Why couldn't she stop listening to it? That crazy little something about Eric made her heart twist and her brain go fuzzy. Always had, which was clear evidence why she needed to focus on how she was going to dig herself out of this Ned Jones debacle rather than call Eric back. They didn't have any other cases in common. He probably wanted to fish a little, find out if she'd followed up on the Drake Thatcher angle yet and get a bead on her plans. She simply wasn't ready to discuss it with opposing counsel even if he did happen to be Eric Nelson, the only guy she'd ever truly opened up to.

With a sigh, she pulled her attention away from Eric's message and confronted the piles of paper-work completely covering her king-size bed. The Jones case files fanned out around her in some sem-blance of chaotic order. She'd gotten comfortable in yoga pants and a fleecy sweatshirt, pushed her hair off her face with a headband, and a fortifying glass of Chianti sat on the nightstand.

In the past two hours, she'd scrawled six pages of notes about every angle of this case, and regardless of Ned Jones's idiotic, shortsighted deal with Drake Thatcher, which he'd laid out for her in detail the other day on digital recording—a cash payoff and a guaranteed position with Thatcher's company if Ned helped take Taka-Hanson down—she still thought she had a shot at winning this thing. It was all about the showdown in the courtroom, right? It may be trumped up, but Taka-Hanson could afford to take the hit.

Why not toss one over for the little guy?

He'd get his money and get out of her hair. She'd make partner as she'd always planned. One case.

One time to focus on the spirit, rather than the letter, of the law. What could it hurt? Certainly Eric's career and Taka-Hanson's booming business would chug right along without a bump. This time, it really was Ned and she who needed the win.

Still, she felt unsettled, conflicted, tense. She wished she could talk to someone about it, but who? No way could she speak to anyone at her firm. To give them the impression that she didn't have this under control would be a disaster. Megan? No. Megan would be horrified to think Colleen would even consider going forward with a "gray area" case. And Mom wouldn't understand the finer points of finessing the law for the greater good either. She'd probably just chide Colleen for working too hard.

Which she had been.

But how else would Colleen ever reach her goals? No one was going to hand her a partnership, tied up in a bow.

Sighing, she rested her back against the sumptuous suede upholstered headboard, pulled her knees up to her chest, and sipped her wine.

The truth? She wanted to talk to Eric.

But she wanted him *not* to be opposing counsel.

Dilemma.

As things stood, she couldn't risk exposing her plans to him. Couldn't risk telling him what Jones had confessed. Couldn't risk…herself. Eric was defending Taka-Hanson, for goodness' sake, and as much as her heart said, "let your guard down," her brain kept whispering, "stay smart." Eric might seem sweet now, but she had to remember how much he disliked her in law school.

Well, at least…after that magical night.

He hadn't disliked her at all until she'd cruelly shoved him aside. Her doing, all of it. She groaned. Her entire life felt like a maze of smoke and mirrors.

To hell with it. Maybe she just wanted to talk to Eric. Needed to. Was that so wrong? Attorney to attorney, person to person, old friend to old friend.

Former lover to former lover.

She didn't have to discuss the Ned Jones debacle in order to hear Eric's voice, right? He obviously needed a call back from her anyway, about some supposedly unrelated case. What the heck?

A deep yearning opened up inside her, like a day lily at the first break of sun. She hadn't realized how utterly alone she'd felt in her career, in her whole *life* until Eric turned up again. Now that isolation was like molten soul magma, deep below the hard surface of her reality, bubbling closer and closer to the top.

Just call him.

She gulped a bit more liquid courage, unwilling

to examine why she needed it, then dialed his home number with icy cold fingers. It rang three times before going to voice mail. Voice mail! After all that anticipation. Disappointment hung on her like a wet veil until it struck her.

Friday night.

Any self-respecting Nelson boy would be at the requisite family dinner, and even though Eric dreaded them, hated debating with his dad and brothers, she knew he'd never let his mom down. Frankly, as much as he bemoaned the mandatory Nelson events, Colleen had always envied him the loud, supposedly chaotic family get-togethers. She imagined bountiful holiday dinners filled with warmth and laughter, shared stories and games and challenges. She imagined driving home with her stomach full, ears buzzing in the silence after the cacophony, a smile on her face. She imagined *belonging*.

As the only child of a single mother, family held a completely different meaning for her. There were no debating brothers or sisters, no aunts, uncles, cousins. No grandparents. Not even a father. Holidays had been something to dread, loaded with stuffed-full silences, melancholy, the knowledge that her mother always wanted something more than just her.

She'd never been enough, in so many ways.

And, although they peacefully coexisted now, the nitrogen sting of those childhood memories had left a frozen spot on her soul.

But the Nelsons.

Ah, the Nelsons.

How different she imagined life was for them.

Colleen would score points for calling Eric at his parents' house. It would give him an excuse to step away from the fracas and discuss business in some quiet room apart from the others. Why she yearned to score points with Eric Nelson wasn't something she wanted to examine at the moment.

With another gulp of wine, she dialed his cell phone quickly, before her bravado fled. The moment she heard the ringing, her breathing shallowed. She laid a palm against her solar plexus and pressed.

Why? Why did he have this effect on her?

Why couldn't she just leave it alone?

Because of one crazy-wonderful night a zillion years ago that had resulted in heartbreak and estrangement, sadness and regret? She'd been impervious to every other guy before and since. Every guy except…him.

"Nelson," he answered, all business despite it being a Friday night.

Colleen fought the urge to giggle. Had to be the

wine; she was *not* a giggler. "Eric? It's Colleen. I'm sorry to call you so late—"

"Oh, hey! No, it's perfect timing, trust me. Hang on." His words were muffled as he spoke to—she assumed—his family. She imagined a fire crackling in the hearth, warm brandy, soft music. Or a ball game, replete with bowls of popcorn and cold beer. All of it sounded wonderful.

Moments passed, then he said, "Okay, I'm here."

Somehow, just hearing his voice eased her omnipresent tension. It had been that way since the first time they'd met at school. She realized, again, how many personality traits he had in common with Megan. "You're at dinner, aren't you?"

"Yes, but we're finished eating. You couldn't have picked a better time to call. My brothers were launching into a debate on the merits and/or shortcomings of—get this—the World Poker Tour, of all god-awful things."

She laughed. "Your brothers sound like a lot of fun."

"It doesn't surprise me that you'd think so. I bet you could give them a run for their money."

"Probably." Colleen didn't want Eric's brothers. She wanted him. "Anyway, I got your message. Something about a case?" She stretched her legs out on her paper-strewn bed, ignoring the crinkling and the yellow highlighter pen poking her in the thigh.

"Yes."

She could hear him settling in, too, and wondered where he was in the house. A crazy part of her wanted to ask. She'd never been to his parents' house, but she still had a picture in her mind.

"Do you remember a sweet older lady by the name of Esther Wellington?" Eric asked.

Colleen's attention spiked. She'd wanted to handle that case so badly, but the partners said no, much to her dismay. It had taken a pair of strappy Manolo stilettos to soothe her anger that time, and, boy, would Framus and the gang have ammo to use against her alleged suitability if they knew *that*. "Of course. Why do you ask?"

"I'm representing her and the group. I know you worked on the case for a bit."

She detected zero judgment in his words. "I tried to."

"Shot down?"

Her self-protective gates rose automatically. "It wasn't right for the firm at the time." God, she sounded like one of their robots. She should've just said yes, the old boys' club shot her down.

"I understand," Eric said, mildly, not pressing her any further, which she appreciated. "Any chance you'd have some time to give me the lowdown on the contractor? I really want to do right by Esther."

Colleen squeezed her eyes closed and tried to ignore the slamming wash of affection for Eric. She should have known he'd help the seniors, regardless of what might be "right" for *his* firm at the time. Eric Nelson was just that kind of guy, and she envied him both the guts and the freedom. When had she become so blinded? Such a puppet? She swallowed back any bit of softness that might come through in her tone. "What do you want to know?"

"Any and every little thing that might help me knock the bastard down hard," Eric said. "A contractor who'd take advantage of a sweetheart like Esther?"

"I know," she said, through clenched teeth.

"You agree?"

"Wholeheartedly."

"Great. So you don't have any problems helping me?"

"Anything you need, Eric. Just…do me a favor."

"Name it."

"Don't call me at my firm about it, okay?"

"What, did Framus bug your phone line? I wouldn't put it past the guy."

She felt like a teenager busting curfew, which pissed her off. How humiliating to have to admit it. But she never knew when someone would be snooping on her at the office. She had a zero level of comfort there. "We're on opposing sides of the Jones case, that's all. I don't want to give any indication of impropriety whatsoever. So just call me at home."

"Fair enough."

She rattled off her number. "And you already have my cell number. Either of those is fine."

"Done. Any other rules?" he said playfully.

"Actually, yes. We agree not to discuss the Jones case while working on the Wellington case." They'd be talking about the Jones case soon enough from opposite sides of the courtroom. She didn't want to talk about the upcoming hearing.

"Okay."

"And we meet on neutral territory."

He laughed softly. "We're not exactly meeting for a gang rumble, Coll. Don't tell me you've started watching *West Side Story* obsessively again."

He remembered her favorite movie from law school, which made her tummy flop. "Oh, be quiet. You love the movie, too," she said, in a wine-induced teasing tone.

"I did have fun watching it with you," he said, in a level, unreadable tone.

What did *that* mean?

"I'm just trying to keep things professional, circumstances being what they are," she said. "If you're okay with those terms—"

"I'm okay with any terms as long as we help Esther Wellington. So you've got yourself a deal, Delaney."

"Okay." She exhaled as quietly as possible. "Good. Great. When do you want to meet?"

"The sooner the better."

Her heart bounced and twirled, like a dancer. "I have time tomorrow. Early afternoon? Late morning?"

"Late morning works for me. Where?"

It had to be somewhere safe, a place where she'd be certain none of her colleagues would spot them. "Where do you live?"

"You want to come to my place?" he asked, sounding slightly astonished.

"N-no," she stammered. "I didn't mean that—"

"It's fine if you do."

"No. I'm in the Gold Coast. Somewhere near both of us is fine."

"Well, I'm in Lincoln Park. Near DePaul U."

Perfect. Close enough to her penthouse to make it as easy as possible for them. She pondered feasible locations. Where would McTierney, Framus and the crowd *never* show up? It came to her in a flash. "I don't know about you, but I'm sick to death of this cold. How about the Lincoln Park Conservatory? The Orchid House?" They kept the Orchid House at a steamy eighty degrees year-round, which sounded like heaven to her. Even more heavenly with Eric by her side.

"I can meet you there at…how about ten? If you have time afterward, we can grab lunch at the Bourgeois Pig Cafe. Ever been there?"

"I haven't. Great name, though."

"Great food, too. You'll love the place," he said. "I have to admit, I'm a bit of a regular."

"Eric Nelson, a regular Bourgeois pig. I like that. I think I'll tuck that away for use in the future." She sipped her wine. "So I take it you don't cook?"

A beat passed.

"Hold up. Are we actually having a cordial conversation?" he drawled.

She rolled her eyes, but truth be told, she enjoyed the slightly flirtatious nature of their banter. "Yes, I believe we are."

"Wow. Hang on. Gotta mark this day in my Palm Pilot."

She groaned. "Let it go. Okay?"

"Fine, fine. No, I'm not much of a cook, to answer your question."

"Typical guy."

"Hey, now. That was sexist. Do *you* cook?"

She toyed with lying, but laughed instead. "Okay, got me there. Not really."

He scoffed. "Typical *attorney* is more like it."

"You may be right. This time." Colleen felt a shift, a balance of power between the two of them, a release. But that brass ring of partnership was never far from her mind or her grasp. Maybe if she helped Eric with the Wellington defense, she could justify in her mind going forward with the Jones case, despite what she knew. The average jury would automatically show sympathy to her client, knowing he faced the formidable power of an international corporation. She could finesse this thing to a win.

But could she live with the lie? With knowing she'd put her own career goals ahead of Axelrod's?

A pang of guilt vibrated through her, but she swallowed to still it. She crunched a fist full of silk comforter in one hand. "Seriously, I hope you fry that contractor's ass, Eric. I really do."

"With your insight, I'm sure I can." His tone lowered into something silky and intimate that touched her deep inside, warmed the cold places and made her feel somehow more whole. "We always did make a good team, you know."

Her chest fluttered, and she glanced at her bedside clock to calculate exactly how many hours until she'd see Eric again. "Well, I don't want to keep you from your family gig. See you tomorrow, okay?"

"Looking forward to it."

Colleen could tell from his tone, he really meant it.

Which meant more to her than he could ever know.

Chapter Six

After speaking to Eric, Colleen wrestled with her bedsheets all night, repeatedly jolted from sleep by dream snippets she couldn't quite recall. The moment her eyes popped open, the dream details fled, but the murky remnants of them left her unsettled and awake far too early. If only she could remember the gist of the dreams. Megan always said they dredged up important messages from the subconscious. Any significance to the fact that Colleen couldn't remember anything? An uncooperative subconscious mind, or a lack of important messages?

Or worse?

Resignedly, she threw back the covers at dawn, showered, and crept out of the house before her mother roused. She didn't want to converse with Mom this morning.

Solitude. Thinking time. That's what Colleen craved.

She needed to sort out her restless feelings.

Where better to get in touch with her own brain than within the verdant, wild beauty of the Lincoln Park Conservatory? Deep down, she aspired to a life of verdant, wild beauty, but she had no idea how to get there or what that actually meant in practical terms. It was probably too late for her anyway, but the notion sure sounded appealing.

Colleen entered the conservatory, along with a few other early birds, when it opened at nine. Her goal—because setting one each morning was a habit she couldn't quite break, even on her days off—was to purge her mind of last night's disturbing lack of sleep before she met up with Eric at ten. Taking a full sixty minutes to indulge in pure sensory stimulation for no other reason than a brain dump?

Heavenly.

She rarely allowed herself the luxury. Today, she planned to revel in it. She had promised her mom she'd do something fun, after all. Of course, enjoying herself alone brought up guilt that she hadn't agreed to her mom's olive branch suggestion that the two of them should do something fun together, but Colleen couldn't think about that right now.

Dissatisfaction.

Guilt.

Remorse.

She desperately needed to wind her way out of this labyrinth of negativity before she lost herself completely and forever. The steamy tropical atmosphere of the Orchid House wrapped her in safety. As she walked slowly through, admiring the exotic orchids, bromeliads and other plants, she practiced Megan's deep-breathing techniques. It helped to center her, to pull the scents of loamy soil, blossoms and moisture into her soul. All that, combined with the beauty of the Victorian peaked glass ceilings and the winding red paths that led her to one surprise vignette after the other, created a magical atmosphere that carried her straight out of her cold Chicago winter survival mind-set, out of her disconcerting dreamscape, into something calmer, more languid.

She felt like a woman for once, not a lawyer.

And, for once, that wasn't a bad thing.

How had that happened?

Pensive, she trailed her fingers along the silky soft

petals of a purple spotted orchid. When exactly had thinking of herself as a woman turned into a bad thing? Law school? Not then, although a few seeds had been planted. They hadn't fully sprouted, however, until she signed on with McTierney, Wenzel, Scott and Framus. Working with the boys' club had slowly chipped away at her sense of self, until she was left with a distorted view of what constituted…well, everything.

Self-image, success, womanhood.

What was success, really?

And who exactly was Colleen Delaney?

A shell. Nothing more.

She felt as if she'd sold her soul to a dark power and hadn't even seen it coming. Now she was stuck treading fetid water in some horrible underworld sea, but maintaining her lifestyle depended on paddling, paddling, paddling. So she was stuck. The ultimate catch-22.

But she didn't want to think about work, the Jones case, her mother or any of the difficult decisions she probably needed to face. This was supposed to be *her* time. She wanted to enjoy her surroundings and revel in the fact that she just might be able to help Esther Wellington after all, in some small way. A subtle smackdown to the partners at her firm. If nothing else, that should boost her spirits.

She wished she were strong enough to simply

leave, find a firm that fit her better. But she'd worked so hard and had become so entrenched in her position, the thought of starting over was as bad as sticking it out where she was. She had financial obligations, the responsibility for her mother. The whole big mess was too much to contemplate in the middle of an important case.

Tranquility eventually eased the knots in her shoulders and dampened the pounding in her temples. She claimed a tucked-away bench and began sifting through her notes on the Esther Wellington case. Even after breaking the news to the woman that she wouldn't be able to represent her, Colleen hadn't been able to part with her notes. A fortuitous turn of events, as it turned out. And yet, the more she delved into the files and thought about Eric taking Esther's case without hesitation, the harder it was to ignore all the dark and empty corners in her life.

Was that what her subconscious had dredged up in her dreams last night? Her many deficits?

She wanted to take on meaningful pro bono work, to make a difference for people like Esther. And, although she wasn't the sort of woman who *needed* a man, *needed* to be in love, she wouldn't mind a little human affection now and then. Some laughter, intimate conversation.

She wouldn't mind some hot sex.

She wouldn't mind, she realized, having a life. It had been so long since she'd felt truly alive. She'd been sleepwalking through her days and nights, but until Eric had reappeared in her world, she hadn't recognized it. Unable to concentrate, and worried that she'd lose the mellowness she'd attained, she set her case notes aside to just take in the gardens for a moment, one that stretched out until she blissfully lost track of time.

The ring of her cell phone startled her into the present, the shrill sound oddly incongruent with the peaceful surroundings. She dug the phone out of her handbag, checked it, and actually smiled at the screen. Eric. Flipping her hair aside, she held it to her ear. "Hey."

"Where are you?"

"On a bench next to the—" she leaned forward and read a small sign "—Rumrilla Sugar Baby."

"Alrighty then, honey bunch, I'm walking past the Bates Fountain right now," he teased.

"Amusing," she said, in a droll tone. But she couldn't miss the flip-flop of her tummy.

"Hey, you used a term of endearment first. Just following your lead."

Colleen rolled her eyes, smiling despite herself. "It's the name of the plant, Nelson."

"Right," he deadpanned, not the least bit apologetic. "My mistake."

She felt happier and lighter than she had in weeks, just hearing his voice. But she didn't know if that was a good thing or a bad thing. Was she pathetic? Was she her mother's daughter? "Do you know how to get here? Through the formal French gardens, and—"

"I'm well acquainted with the Orchid House. I've been here many times."

"Really."

"You sound surprised."

"I guess I am, a little. Though I don't know why." Eric Nelson was a flower fan. Not that big of a departure for the guy she used to know, she supposed. "Well…great, then. I'll see you soon? The weather's gorgeous inside."

"I'll be there in moments. Warm the bench for me."

Colleen ended the phone call realizing one more thing in this morning rife with epiphanies. She didn't want to be a benchwarmer in life anymore. She'd been doing it for far too long, and as a result, her world felt off-kilter, unbalanced, unfulfilled. She was so far gone, she didn't know how to get back to that center, where she knew who she was and why she wanted the things she did. The thought of overhauling her life overwhelmed her.

Baby steps, Megan would say. One small bit at a time.

Maybe repairing the friendship she once had with Eric was the first step to a series of changes Colleen needed to make, and maybe today was the day. She mentally shredded her *all business* mantra. Today, no matter how scary, she'd challenge herself to move beyond that. What exactly that would entail, she didn't know. But she felt ready to leap and wait for the net to appear.

Waiting for Eric to appear turned out to be a scarier, albeit more exciting, prospect. She glanced down the winding path, first in one direction, then the other, as anticipation built in her middle. When he rounded a curve of greenery and came into view, she couldn't prevent the sharp inhale. The man enthralled her. Pure and simple. Vying for nonchalance, she raised a hand.

Eric's smile made his eyes gleam. "There you are," he said, dropping onto the bench next to her. "I was about to do the Marco Polo thing via cell phone. This place is a maze."

"I didn't want to move from the—" she indicated the sign "—*sugar baby*. Thought it might throw you off."

He leaned in and read the sign. "Damn. So you really didn't call me a sweet name."

She chuckled. "I really didn't. Sorry."

"Oh, well. A guy can dream, right?"

Colleen's face heated, and she let her gaze drop to the files on her lap. God, had she completely forgotten how to harmlessly flirt with a man?

Or was it just *this* man?

Eric seemed to pick up on her discomfort. "So what do you have for me?"

Back onto safe territory.

She patted the stack of folders. "Quite a bit, actually. I delved pretty far into the case before I had to let it go." She handed the paperwork to him, and watched as he flipped through quickly.

"Wow. This isn't preliminary research."

"No."

"You truly worked this case."

She twisted her lips to the side. "I tried."

He studied her, then laid a palm gently on her forearm. "What really happened, Coll? Friend to friend. I'm sure you've researched my background now. You know I'm not trying to get dirt to use against you later."

Her shoulders sagged. It wasn't as if her firm's reputation was a secret. "The partners aren't really big on pro bono." Especially not if Colleen was the attorney making the request. "They're much more fond of billable hours."

"I figured that was it."

"I wanted to help her, Eric. I did."

"I can see that from all you gathered." He huffed, shaking his head with disgust. "Money-grubbing bastards. Don't they see the benefits of giving back to the community?"

Colleen realized anew what an alternate universe she worked in. How had she been so blind? "I'm not sure they care. It's definitely not part of the firm's unwritten mission statement, not that they've actually let me read the apparently supersecret mission statement. Different story, though." A pause fell between them with an emotional thud. Colleen swallowed, then gestured to her research. "Anyway, I hope you can use it."

He scanned her notes. "It's a solid bet that the contractor's going down. And your work will help me accomplish that so much quicker." For a moment, they sat in companionable silence, taking in the calming effects of the gardens. Or, Eric enjoyed the gardens while Colleen shored up the nerve to do something she should've done years ago.

Baby steps.

Deep breath in...eased out. "Eric? I'm sorry."

"You have nothing to apologize for. If your supervisors won't let you take a case—"

"That's not what I'm sorry for." As boldly as she

could, she met his gaze, watched his Adam's apple rise and fall on a swallow.

"Then, what?" he asked quietly, as if not wanting to break the spell they seemed to be under.

"Us. How I treated you…after."

A beat passed. "Aw, Colleen," Eric said, his voice laced with regret. He put his arm around her and pulled her closer. "It's okay."

She rested her head on his shoulder, mostly because that meant she didn't have to look into his face. She had to say this, get it out. The words, however, were excruciating. "It's not okay. The night we…that we…you and I—"

"I know the night, Coll."

"Right. Well, it was…beautiful. Unimaginable."

"Earth-shattering?"

"That, too."

"Glad it wasn't only earth-shattering for me."

"It scared me," Colleen admitted.

She felt his sigh more than heard it. "Why?"

"Long story for another time. But I shouldn't have treated you the way I did, regardless of my fear."

"It's really okay. Happened a long time ago."

"Please, just listen. You made me feel amazing, and amazing about myself, which is rare."

Eric rested his cheek on her head. "You should feel amazing about yourself every day."

"Yeah, sure. I'm a mess." More than he knew.

"You're fine. I mean, granted, you work for idiots, but you? Top shelf, Coll. Always have been."

She huffed her disbelief, not about to run off a litany of her shortcomings. "Anyway, I'm sorrier than you know. You were never anything but good to me, and I took that for granted then threw it away. I guess I didn't realize how special a person you are."

"Hey, you didn't throw it away altogether. I'm right here, right now, aren't I?"

"That's different. I guess I'm just saying, I hope we can be friends again. Truce?"

"Truce." Abruptly, Eric pulled away from her, but he gripped her elbow and his eyes gleamed. "What are you doing today?"

"Um, well—"

"I mean, for the rest of the day."

She considered making an excuse, fleeing, avoiding the danger of him. But she was tired of that. Hadn't she vowed to leap today? "Actually, nothing."

"Let's spend the day together. It'll be our little ritual to bury the past."

She hesitated for a moment, then laughed, in spite of herself. So much like Megan, this guy. She simply couldn't stop noticing that. "Fine. What do you want to do?"

"Anything. Nothing. I don't care." His tone lowered into a huskier version of itself, and he ran the backs of his fingers down her cheek. "I've missed you. Missed your friendship and the times we used to spend together just talking. We can do...whatever."

She pondered the dazzling array of options in front of them. "I can't risk running into anyone from my firm. I know that seems so juvenile, but with the Jones case—"

"No explanation necessary. We'll leave the city."

"O-okay."

"Where do you want to go?"

She crossed her arms and considered the question. If she could go anywhere, do anything with Eric Nelson...? It came to her in a flash. "You want the truth?"

"No," he said, in a droll tone. "I love it when women lie to me."

She smacked him playfully in the arm, then tossed her hair and tried for brave. "Okay. I want to go to Schaumburg. To your parents' house."

Eric pulled back in disbelief. "What? It's supposed to be a fun day. Really?"

"Yes, really. And it will be fun. I've heard about the infamous Nelson family dinners for years. I want to see where they happen, give myself a frame of reference."

"Well, okay," he said, his tone dubious. "You may regret this. The Nelson family can drain the life out of you before you realize what's happening."

"No worries." She stood, shouldered her purse. "My firm already sucked the life out of me, so I'm an empty shell." She didn't miss the line of concern that bisected his brows, and she flipped away his worry with one hand. "It's okay. At least for today, I don't care. Show me where you grew up, where you went to high school, where you had your first kiss. I want to meet your mom and see your childhood bedroom."

The interest in his eyes sparked. "My childhood bedroom, huh? Now that sounds like fun."

She scoffed. "Don't be insane. It's your parents' *house.* That's not what I meant."

"A guy's gotta dream, Colleen," he said, before draping his arm casually over her shoulder and steering her toward the exit.

"You dream a little bit too much, I think," she told him, with feigned primness. Deep inside, however, she hoped all his dreams were about her.

"Probably true. Besides, it wouldn't be as titillating as one would hope. Mom finally accepted the fact that I wasn't coming home and turned it into a scrapbooking room."

They left the gardens arm in arm, laughing.

Now this, Colleen thought, was fun.

* * *

Eric couldn't expose the level of nervousness he felt about bringing Colleen to his parents' house. His mother would think he and Colleen were dating and ask all kinds of invasive questions. His dad would draw him into some sort of embarrassing and meaningless debate. Odds were, Brian and his wife, Melody, would be there, too. Innuendo and assumptions would zing through the Nelson clan quicker than a series of lightning strikes from a single storm supercell.

Colleen didn't know what she was in for. On the other hand, the thought of his family pairing him with Colleen in their minds held the kind of appeal he didn't dare raise his hopes about, despite her heartfelt apology. Not with all he knew about Colleen.

Friendship was one thing. More? Too much to wish for.

They passed the water tower announcing their entry into Schaumberg, and he killed as much time as possible dashing from elementary school to high school to first kiss to first breakup—even first job, at the chicken-wing restaurant that was now a Chinese take-out place called Wok On In. He crawled past the old Schaumburg airport and crept around Volkening Lake. He even showed her the giant red kettle grill in front of the Weber Grill Restaurant. Eighteen years of his life summed up with a few select pins in the map of his youth. Crazy.

Finally, when he could stall no longer, he turned onto his parents' street and slowed to a crawl. "You sure you want to do this?"

"Of course. I'm excited."

He bugged his eyes at her. "How could you possibly be excited about seeing my boring childhood home?"

"That's just it." She cast about for the correct words. "You *have* a childhood home whereas we moved a zillion times. It's such a foreign concept to me, returning to one's roots. I always wanted— Never mind."

She'd stopped herself so abruptly, Eric did a double take. "Always wanted what?"

"Nothing. It's not important. The point is, Counselor, you let me pick the day's activities, and right now, I just want to see how the other half lived. Case closed."

Someday, he'd find out more about how she grew up. "Fine, you win. The other half lived in suburban dullness," he said, pulling into his parents' driveway. "Voila. This is it. Can we leave now?"

She studied the house with such raw yearning on her face, it tugged at his heart. He wanted desperately to pull her into his arms.

"No way. We're here." She hiked her shoulders and let them drop. "We might as well go all the way."

He leered. "Is this a veiled reference to my childhood bedroom again?"

"Cut it out, Nelson. *Cut.* Get it? *That* was a reference to the fact that it's now a categorically unromantic scrapbooking room," she said, her words laced with laughter. "I want an inside view of the Nelson family enclave. I do not want to defile your mother's crafting space. *Friends,* remember?"

"Another dream dashed." He cut the engine. "And *christen* is the word you're thinking of, I believe. Not *defile.*"

Her eyes widened with disbelief, but he could tell she was teasing. "You mean you've never had sneaky sex in your childhood bedroom?"

"You're a nut job," he said. "No. I'm not that sly. I would've been busted immediately."

"That's what makes it fun. The risk."

"Well, who knew, Delaney? I'm learning something new about you every moment."

"Be quiet. Come on. Let's go in."

He glanced toward the house with mock dread and remorse. "You asked for this, so here we go."

"I'm ready. Can't wait." She rubbed her palms together, then reached for the door handle.

"Why do you have such a problem with your family?"

"You know all this, Coll—"

"Tell me again. It's been a while."

"It's not that I don't love them. But they're...exhausting. They debate, they one-up each other, they embarrass me at every opportunity. I don't know, they're..."

"Family, Eric. They're family. And you're not like them, but that's okay. They're still your family."

"I suppose you're right."

He touched her arm. "Hang on. You do realize, the simple act of bringing you here is going to set off a heat rash of rumors within the 'Nelson family enclave,' as you put it. Prepared for that?"

She blinked. "You mean they'll think we're dating?"

"Uh, yep."

She seemed to consider that, but only briefly. "I'm sure you'll disabuse them of the notion in short order. Let's go inside."

"You're the boss." Eric followed Colleen up the winding slate path to the house thinking, perhaps, he wouldn't be so quick to disabuse his family of any notions they might concoct. The idea of being associated with Colleen in people's minds grew more appealing by the minute, no matter how far from the truth it may be.

With a deep breath and a small prayer for strength, Eric leaned in and rang the doorbell.

Chapter Seven

As the sound of footsteps approached from far off within the house, Eric spun toward her. "Rules of thumb, trust me on this. Don't let my mom corner you alone, try not to engage if they force you into a debate of any kind, and feel free not to answer questions that make you uncomfortable."

Colleen grinned and bounced on her heels. "Wow, I've never seen you lose your cool like this, Nelson. This is going to be the most fun I've had in a while."

"You have to understand. My family—"

The door swung open.

Colleen watched him whip back to face the shapely, fiftysomething woman who'd appeared, blinking with surprise, in the doorway. She had the same dark blond hair and chocolate-brown eyes as Eric, but her heart-shaped face and slightly tilted eyes lent a softer, more elfin note to her overall appearance. Eric must've gotten the rugged bone structure from dear ol' dad, Colleen mused.

"Why, Eric! What a lovely surprise."

"Mom, hey." He aimed a thumb over his shoulder at his car. "We can leave if we're interrupting—"

"Are you kidding? Not at all. It's so nice to see you outside the Forcible Friday Feast, since we rarely *do*," she said wryly, driving home the subtle mom-guilt point as she reached out a fine-boned hand toward Colleen's. Once she'd grasped it, she smiled at Colleen, gently pulling her over the threshold into the house. "Hello to you, too, dear," she said, drawing out her words. "Eric never mentioned a lady friend. And you are?"

Wow, Eric had a point. Sweet as Mrs. Nelson was, this did sort of feel like being sucked into a vortex. Colleen hardly had time to take in the decor, but she could smell woodsmoke and something baking. Possibly cookies. The vortex seemed friendly enough. "I'm Colleen Delaney, Mrs. Nelson. Eric and I are...we, uh—"

"We went to law school together," Eric interjected, from behind her, saving her the awkwardness of explaining their inexplicable relationship. "And we happened to run into each other recently."

"I see, and you somehow wound up in Schaumburg at the Nelson homestead. Hmm," Mrs. Nelson said, humming her curiosity with a heavy dose of innuendo. She pulled Colleen closer, tucking her arm into Colleen's elbow. "So you're an attorney as well?"

"Yes, ma'am."

"How lovely. Do the two of you work together?"

"No," Colleen and Eric said, in unison. Colleen glanced at him, then added, "Different firms."

"Ah. The legal community's a small world, I suppose. Even Melody—" she tapped Colleen's forearm "—our daughter-in-law, married to Eric's youngest brother, Brian—"

"She knows, Mom," Eric said.

One of Mrs. Nelson's well-groomed brows rose with interest. "Yes, well, Melody works as a receptionist in a law firm and runs a legal gossip blog on the side, although that's a big secret."

Colleen blinked at her. "Oh, my gosh, is it *that* gossip site?" Colleen had to admit, reading the snarky Web site was a guilty pleasure.

"CaughtInYourBriefs.com. That's the one. But—" the older woman laid one index finger across her lips "—mum's the word. Melody's anonymous for a reason."

"My lips are sealed," Colleen said. She threw Eric a *you never told me that* glance, which he answered with a sheepish shrug. It was her fault as much as his, really. She could've asked him the name of the site when he'd mentioned his sister-in-law ran a gossip blog, but she'd been too focused on the Jones case.

"Well, come in, come in, take your coats off. Dad and Brian are watching the Huskies game in the family room, Eric," she said, referring to Northern Illinois University's team, "so you go on in and join them. Melody and I were chatting in the kitchen. I'll just take Colleen and—"

"No, that's okay," Eric said. "I don't feel like watching the game. I'll come with you."

Colleen had to admit, relief spiraled through her. Especially knowing that Melody ran that site. Every attorney she knew both read and denounced the thing. It was more alluring than the biggest celebrity scandal rags, but no one wanted to be on it.

Mrs. Nelson stopped, lowered her chin, scrutinized her son. "You don't feel like watching the Huskies? That's a first."

"First time for everything," Eric said, in a level tone.

"Hmm." His mother pierced him with a measuring stare that actually made Colleen gulp, then leaned in toward Colleen and resumed the path toward the kitchen. "Boys. Who can figure them out?"

"Not me."

"He must not want to leave your side. So cute." And then a bit louder, in a singsong tone, "Never knew you were such a romantic, Eric, dear. He's never brought a woman home, you know. So I guess there *is* a first time for everything."

Colleen stifled a laugh and flashed a sympathetic glance over her shoulder toward Eric, who really did appear grim. Poor guy. He hadn't been kidding about the assumptions and innuendos. They didn't detract from the warmth of his mother's welcome, however, in which Colleen reveled.

Once they were seated around the vast, granite island in the bright, warm kitchen, coffee and cookies in front of them, young Melody leaned toward Colleen with a gleam in her eye.

"So you have to tell us. How long have you and Eric been dating? I mean, this is big news in the Nelson circle. Freaking huge news. I can hardly keep from texting the other brothers right this very minute."

Colleen's nape prickled and her mouth fell open.

She had to remember who she was speaking to and never drop her guard. She shot a glance toward Eric to find him wearing a similar expression. Thankfully, he recovered more quickly than she did.

"Leave the woman alone, Mel," Eric chastised. "Mom, you, too. I didn't bring Colleen here for you to interrogate her, for Pete's sake."

Colleen reached out and laid her hand on Eric's forearm. "It's okay. Really."

"We're not interrogating, Eric," Melody said.

"Whatever. Stop probing. You'll scare her away," Eric continued, his face reddened.

"Scare her!" his mom exclaimed.

"We're not scary, we're family," Melody said. "Colleen, are we scary?"

After a moment of breath holding, Colleen released a nervous laugh on a whoosh. "Not scary exactly. But I come from a very, very small family. In fact, it's just Mom and me." She crinkled her nose. "So maybe a tad different from what I'm used to."

"See?" Eric said, spreading his arms wide. "It's like being hit with a steamroller walking into this joint. And you wonder why I don't bring women home."

Unbidden, Colleen's stomach soured. She didn't really know much about Eric Nelson, come to think of it. Was he dating someone? Several someones? Ugh. She couldn't dwell on it. "It's okay," Colleen said in a rush, curling her hands around the warm coffee mug. "I like it. You have a very welcoming family and home, Mrs. Nelson."

The older woman waved her delicate hand. "Oh, enough of the formalities. Call me Emily, for good-ness' sake. You make me feel ninety years old with that Mrs. Nelson stuff."

"Emily it is," Colleen said, with a nod.

Eric stood. *"Emily,"* he said pointedly. "Mel? I'm going to show Colleen around the house for a bit so you can have time to sharpen your fangs and talons."

Emily hiked an eyebrow. Melody picked up a warm cookie from the cooling rack and bonked it off his forehead.

Miraculously, he caught it, winked, took a bite. "Nice throw, sis."

"Oh, be quiet," Melody said, the affection peek-ing through her pout. "We will get all the info on your relationship one way or another, so deal with it."

Alarm sirens wailed in Colleen's head. Family or not, Colleen couldn't risk ending up on Melody's Web site. She grabbed her own cookie and tried to smooth over Eric's snarky tone by bestowing her most blazing smile on the Nelson matriarch. "Thank you so much for letting me just drop in," she gushed. Wow, she was totally out of her attorney element here. "Eric's told me all about your scrapbooking room. I can't wait to see it."

"Hmm, you know, that used to be Eric's bedroom." Emily tapped her chin with one finger, feigning disapproval, but a sparkle in her eyes told Colleen she was teasing—mostly to antagonize her son. "Years ago, I wouldn't allow any of my darling boys to take girls into their bedrooms unsupervised. I don't know…"

"Bye, Mom," Eric said, with the utmost sarcastic patience. "See you in a few."

He grabbed Colleen's hand which, admittedly, felt perfect to her, and perfectly natural. They walked in silence through the neat, suburban home, and Colleen soaked it in. Most of the decor hadn't been updated for a decade or more. The kitchen had obviously been redone, but the rest of the house seemed like your average, middle-class, American family home.

Neat, but lived-in. Old, but loved.

Framed photos angling up the stairway chronicled the lives of the Nelson boys, and the black-and-white wedding photo of Emily and Mr. Nelson stopped Colleen in her tracks. So young. So hopeful. So in love. Had she ever looked like that?

"Mom was a hottie back then, huh?"

"Mmm. Beautiful," Colleen said.

"Who knew she'd mature into such a meddling old—"

"Eric!" But she had to laugh. Eric's affection for his mother, meddler or not, showed in his eyes as they stood side by side studying the wedding photo. Before she had a chance to think it through, she blurted, "Are you dating anyone?"

He did a double take. "Are you asking me out? I thought this was just a friend thing."

She rolled her eyes, but realized belatedly that asking Eric about his private life while looking at a wedding photo of his parents probably hadn't been the wisest of moves. "No. It's just…your mom said you didn't bring women home, and then you said… Never mind."

"No, Coll, I'm not dating anyone," he said lightly. "How about you?"

She scoffed. "Please." Time for a subject change. She turned and observed the lower level from their vantage point on the stairs, and it tugged at her heart.

Wonderfully normal. She loved it.

She'd spent her childhood moving from ratty apartment to slightly nicer apartment—when a man came along for Mom—and back to ratty apartment again. New areas, different schools. She'd never had a bedroom that felt the least bit permanent, and she'd always longed for a house exactly like this one. She'd dreamt about knowing all the neighbors, and who'd lived in their houses before them. About going to school, kindergarten through senior year, with the same group of kids. About taping her Goo Goo Dolls and Duran Duran posters onto bedroom walls she knew were hers forever.

But that hadn't happened. The corners of her posters got ripped farther and farther inward each time she had to tear them from one generic wall and move them to another. She sighed, hating how the depressing memories clung to her like lint on her man-tailored, black wool suit.

Eric looked at her. "You okay?"

"Yeah. I just…I really love it here."

He pulled his chin back. "Oh, come on, Coll. I know the Gold Coast. You probably live in a glitzy high-rise with a view of the water from several rooms. Probably floor-to-ceiling windows. You can't possibly compare that with a circa 1960, middle America suburban split-level."

"As a matter of fact, I do live in a lake-view high-rise, but that's not the point," she said, as they climbed the rest of the stairs that creaked every now and then. He probably knew every creak, having lived within these walls for decades. One of her heartstrings panged and snapped.

"So what's the point?"

At the top of the stairs, she dropped his hand and faced him, spread her arms wide. "This. All of it. You walk in, and it probably smells just like home. The house you grew up in. Right?"

He scrubbed a hand through his hair, leaving it askew. "Well, sure, but—"

"Don't take that for granted, Eric. Some of us never had it. I don't have a childhood home to return to. Or a loud, raucous family who annoys me but always welcomes me in with warmth and food."

"Now, I beg to differ." He held up a finger. "You did, in fact, once mention that your mother annoys you."

"Well, yes, but—" She bit her bottom lip, suddenly flooded with emotion she couldn't quite pinpoint.

Eric dipped down and cupped her elbows, peering into her eyes which most certainly looked watery. "Hey, I didn't mean to upset you."

"No." She gulped. "You didn't."

"Then, what's wrong?"

She cleared her throat, then shook her hair back to regain her composure. "Nothing. Or everything. I'm not sure. All I know is, you have everything here

I ever wanted growing up, and you can't even stand coming home once a week." She sniffed, realizing how stupid she sounded. "I'm sorry. It could be the nightmare this case is turning into that's fraying on my nerves. I really appreciate you bringing me here."

"Okay," he said, still studying her with uncertainty.

"Your family is great, if a little pushy."

He broke a smile.

"Seriously, thank you." The air around them seemed to change, and she couldn't look away from his melted chocolate gaze. Her mouth went dry, and she moistened her lips with a quick flick of her tongue. His eyes dropped to her mouth, and then she knew.

She knew, and she wanted it.

Eric Nelson was going to kiss her, right on the upper stair landing of his childhood home. She lifted her chin and leaned in. Eric moved closer, hesitated. He searched her eyes, then pulled her toward him. Her eyelids closed. She felt his warm breath on her face before lips touched hers, and when they did, it felt like a lightning strike. It had even looked like a lightning strike—a sudden bright flash in the sky.

"Ha!" came Melody's voice.

Eric and Colleen wrenched apart and stared in horror at young Melody waggling her bedazzled camera phone.

"I have the evidence, right here. Eric Nelson and Colleen Delaney locking lips on the staircase. This is *so* going on the blog."

Colleen's stomach collapsed, heavy upon legs that suddenly felt cemented to the floor. *Oh, no.*

This could not happen. How could she have been so utterly weak?

Melody spun and pummeled her way down the stairs, giggling, unaware of the havoc she could wreak by posting that photo. If it actually made it onto the blog and someone from her firm saw it—

"Mel, wait!" Eric said, lunging after her, taking the stairs two at a time.

Frozen, shaking, Colleen stood on the stair landing and covered her face with her palms. She could hear one helluva chase carrying on between brother and sister-in-law below her, but she didn't know what to do. She couldn't move. She very well might've made the *new* stupidest mistake of her career.

"What on earth is going on here?" she heard a booming male voice from below that resembled Eric's. Probably his father's. "Melody, stop running around like a crazy person. You're carrying my grandchild, I might remind you."

Colleen couldn't make out the ensuing argument, but all of a sudden, she felt a light touch on her upper arm. Gasping, she dropped her hands. Emily Nelson stood there, perplexed. "Honey, what happened?"

Colleen couldn't believe it. Her chin actually quivered. It was the nurturing mom thing that undid her. "Melody took a photo of Eric and me. Kissing." Her face flooded with heat. "She said she was going to upload it to the blog."

Emily's expression softened. "Well, that's okay, sweetie. You're both adults. You don't work in the same firm. Kissing often happens when adults are romantically involved."

Strangely, she didn't want to break the spell, didn't want to dispel the illusion that she and Eric were a couple. But she had to tell the truth. Her career could depend on it. "The problem is, Emily, we're not romantically involved."

"I'm sorry?"

"We're opposing counsel on a major case. The biggest case of my career, and I work for a very cut-throat law firm who would not appreciate knowing I spent my Saturday with Eric, no matter how innocent." A tear had the nerve to spill over and tumble down her cheek. She smacked it away. "If anyone there sees that picture, I'll lose my job," she said, her voice husky with shame.

Emily's eyes widened. "Surely not. Over a photo?"

"Trust me," Colleen said.

Emily's expression moved quickly from surprise to confusion to alarm to control, then she grasped Colleen's elbow. "Come on."

The two of them marched down the stairs, and at the bottom, Emily barked, "Melody!"

Chaos stilled. Melody glanced over, wide-eyed, at her mother-in-law. "Yes?"

Emily held her hand out, palm up, and snapped her fingers toward her. "Give up the phone."

"But—"

"Enough of this. If Eric and Colleen want to keep things private, it's our job as family to support them. Family before Web site, not the other way around. Now, hand it over."

Eric, chest still heaving from exertion, cocked his head in Colleen's direction.

She hiked her shoulder, clueless.

Reluctantly, Melody placed the cell phone in Emily's palm. "Sorry, you guys," she said, ducking her head. "I was just messing around. Like, you're both grown up. I didn't know it was such a big deal."

"Dad? Brian?" Emily said. "Awkward moment for an introduction, but this is Colleen, Eric's friend who's come to visit for the first time. And it appears we're acting like hooligans and owe her an apology."

"So what's new?" Brian asked, from his kicked-back position in a recliner. "Hey, Colleen."

"Hello," she managed, though her heart still pounded up near her throat.

Brian grinned, then gave Eric a thumbs-up. Melody sank onto her husband's lap.

Eric's dad, a strapping, thicker version of his son with—as predicted—the same chiseled features, leveraged himself from his chair and crossed the room. "Colleen, is it?"

"Y-yes."

"Robert Nelson, but everyone calls me Dad. I apologize, though I don't know what for. I was engrossed in the game. In the Nelson household, though, it's often wise to offer a blanket apology to newcomers."

Colleen smiled. "You look like Eric."

"Sure, about forty pounds and twenty years ago."

"More like fifty/thirty," Eric said.

Dad glowered at him, then held out a hand for Colleen to shake, which she did. "So nice to meet you. You're always welcome in our zoo, at your own peril."

"Thank you. And you don't owe me an apology. No one does." She saw Melody peer up from under the shame veil of her lashes, and she smiled at the younger woman. "It's okay. Really."

Emily handed the cell phone to Colleen. "I don't have the foggiest idea how to mess with pictures on a telephone, for heaven's sake. If you want to delete it—"

"Aw, but it's a great photo," Melody said. "I won't post it anywhere, I promise. You guys should have it, though."

"That's okay, Mel," Eric said. "Really. We don't need the photo."

Emily added, "Melody, dear, let them decide when and how and to whom they announce whatever relationship they have, okay? I'll explain later. Or Eric can, if he chooses."

Colleen, meanwhile, had opened the photo, and it stole her breath. The curve of her jawline, Eric's lips on hers, backlit from the ceiling fixture in the hallway behind them like an aura. Feeling only slightly guilty, she sent it to her own phone, then deleted both the photograph and any sign that she'd sent it anywhere. Brash perhaps, but she wanted to look at that photo later.

"Done," she said, with a tight smile. She handed the phone back to Emily, who crossed the room and returned it to a very smacked-down looking Melody.

"I'm really sorry, Colleen. I was just having fun."

"It's okay, sis," Eric said, ruffling her hair. "Sensitive situation, that's all."

Melody's eyes bugged. "Oh, my God. Colleen, are you already married? Is that what's up?"

All the air left Colleen's lungs as if Melody's question were a boot to the gut. Colleen splayed a hand on her chest. "No! No, of course not."

"I swear, Mel, if any of this ends up on that blog—"

"It won't!" Melody flailed her arms wide. "God, Eric! I got the message, loud and clear."

Eric studied her through narrowed eyes for several seconds before easing back.

"Can we all just have a nice visit now, please?" Emily asked, exasperated. "Lord, I've been asking that for decades, and it gets me nowhere."

"Sure, Mom," Eric said, but abruptly focused on his own cell phone. He unhooked it from his belt, read through a text, snapped it closed, and blew out a sigh. "Actually, darn it. Looks like I have to get back to the city. Sorry, Colleen."

"No, that's okay. Is anything wrong?"

He mussed his hair with one palm. "Something came up with a case. No worries."

"On a Saturday?" his mother exclaimed.

"It happens." He strode over, kissed his mom on the cheek, then turned back to the others. "Bye, all."

Everyone called out their goodbyes as Emily bustled off to retrieve Eric's and Colleen's coats.

"We'll be on our best behavior next time you stop by," Eric's father said, with a wink toward Colleen.

"It was lovely to meet you all," Colleen said, and she meant it. The Nelsons might be exuberant, a little overbearing, halfway terrifying at times. But they were alive, pulsating with everything that meant family.

Banter, bickering, baked goods.

Brian and a subdued Melody returned Colleen's kind words, and in a flurry of wool and scarves and icy air, Colleen and Eric were gone.

Chapter Eight

Fuming and humiliated by the spectacle of his family, Eric didn't speak until they got into the car and snapped their seat belts on. He kicked the engine over, cranked up the heat, and blew out a breath on the tail of a particularly ripe swearword. "At least that works every time." He tossed her a sidelong glance.

"What? Swearing?"

"No. The handy dandy fake urgent text message."

Colleen uttered her shock on a laugh, then grinned at him, shaking her head. "You mean, you don't have to get back to the city for a case?"

"No, I had to get out of there before I became a basket case."

"Sneaky move, Counselor."

"I never should have subjected you to them," he muttered, teeth clenched. "I'm sorry."

"Don't be silly. I liked them."

He scoffed.

"No, really." She glanced at the warm glow emanating from the windows of the Nelson's house. "At least your parents' house is lively."

An innocuous opening, one he wasn't going to miss. "What's it like at home with your mom?"

"Well, first of all, it's my house, not hers. So it's different."

"True."

"It's…quiet. We keep to ourselves mostly."

"Why's that?"

"We're just so different, Eric." She sighed. "It's a really long story for another time." Colleen bit her bottom lip. "I'm worried about her. She doesn't go out."

"Ever?"

"Not lately. Not since the knee surgery."

"Well, maybe she just needs time to recuperate."

"It's been over a year. Clean bill of health from the docs and even they're urging her to get out and use the new knee. I think she's depressed, maybe."

"Why?"

Colleen pursed her lips, measuring. "Just a theory, but I think the knee replacement has made her feel old. She needs some incentive to get out and about, but I haven't found it yet."

Eric felt the tension emanating from the passenger side of his car. He stayed quiet. As suspected, Colleen changed the subject.

"Anyway...I can't believe I didn't even get to see the infamous scrapbooking room."

"It's impressive. I'd say there's always next time, but I don't want to throw you back to the wolves."

"The only remotely wolfish fact is that Melody runs CaughtInYourBriefs.com." Colleen shook her head. "I mean, I remember you mentioning she ran some idiotic gossip site during lunch, but I can't believe it's *that* particular one. Why didn't you tell me?"

He tensed at the mere thought. "At that point in our renewed acquaintance? Please. You would've run screaming."

"Okay, you have a point."

"Plus, I try to block it from my conscious mind most of the time anyway, believe me. Melody's site isn't something I'm particularly proud of."

"You must read it, though."

"Sure. What attorney in Chicago doesn't gobble

the thing up? Doesn't mean I want to admit my sister-in-law runs it. I want no connection to that site whatsoever." He laid an arm across the headrest of her seat and twisted around to maneuver backward out of the winding driveway. "I swear, Coll, if I'd had any idea Melody would pull that camera-phone stunt—"

Colleen held up her palms. "No harm, no foul. And I deleted the photo, so there's no harm."

"Thank God. My family is freaking nuts. Now you see why I dread coming here every Friday night."

They drove to the end of the street, took a left, and merged into traffic before Colleen said, "Actually, I don't. Nuts or not, they love you. You always have a place to go where people open the door, hug you, offer you cookies—"

"Torment me, embarrass me."

"That's family." She shrugged. "Doesn't sound so awful to me. Growing up, every single year I asked Santa for…"

"For what?"

She flicked away his question. "Never mind. It's the stupid musings of a little girl. I'm over it."

"Perhaps. But I still want to know."

"Okay, fine." She sighed, wound her hands into a knot on her lap. "I asked for a real family, with a house and a yard, siblings and a mom who wasn't sad and desperate all the time."

Eric's heart squeezed. "Wow."

She twisted her mouth to the side. "I'm sorry, that's probably way too much pathetic information and you're not exactly my therapist."

"No, it's—" The wail of a passing ambulance halted his response. When the lights disappeared in front of them and the only sound was the wipers swishing across the windshield, Eric asked, "Do you still want a family?"

"I have my mom," she said, in a monotone. "I'm trying to stop taking her for granted. You're born into whatever family is meant for you, I guess."

"I meant, a family of your own." Damn it, he couldn't help but imagine beautiful little girls who looked just like Colleen, and maybe one boy with uncooperative sandy-colored hair. Their children.

"I never thought I did," she said, on a sigh.

Her words didn't really answer his question, but then again, the wistful look on her lovely face combined with the cryptic statement answered more than she realized. He decided to let it rest.

She tucked her hair behind her ears. "So... speaking of family and Web sites and such, Melody's got to have some excellent dirt on you. Why haven't you ever ended up on the blog?"

"Frequent death threats," he said.

She eyed him sideways, then laughed. "Excellent." They drove in silence until the water tower faded in the distance. "Bye, Schaumburg," she said, with a wave.

"You sound like you'll miss it."

"I will. It was fun." She took in a breath and held it for a moment. On the exhale, she asked, "Does this mean our day together is over?"

A beat passed. He swallowed thickly. "Do you want it to be?"

She considered the question. "Honestly? No. I'm having too good of a time. I haven't thought about that idiot Ned Jones for hours."

Alert. Eric pressed his lips together to keep from commenting. He'd agreed they wouldn't talk about the case, and he wasn't going to be the one to breach that. But he wondered why the client whose honor she so vehemently defended a couple weeks ago was suddenly "that idiot Ned Jones." Could she have confirmed his hunch about the Drake Thatcher connection?

He made a mental note to hit the research full force on Monday, then simply said, "I'm having fun, too, now that we're no longer at my parents' house. And I've still got steam if you do."

"Power on," she said, pumping her fist.

He reached over and squeezed her leg briefly. "What's next on the agenda, then?"

"Well…if you don't mind, we should pick up my car. I don't particularly want to leave it in the conservatory parking lot."

"Not a problem. And after that?"

She seemed to morph into a shy version of the Colleen he knew, which left him intrigued.

She tucked her hair behind her ears. "If the offer still stands, I'd love to see your place."

He shot her a double take. "My— Really?" He sent up a silent prayer of thanks that his cleaning lady had come around earlier that day to de-guy the house.

"You sound surprised."

"Frankly, I am. But, don't get me wrong, I'm not at all devastated by the notion."

"Good, then. It's a plan." She curled one delicate hand around the seat belt crisscrossing her body. "Moving forward with the plans, logistically, we'll probably have to eat at some point."

He balked. "I'm not cooking. I don't even really know how to operate my stove. Possibly the instruction manual and warranty card still reside inside the thing, but that's unconfirmed."

"No problem. I'm not cooking either. Takeout?"

"Sounds good. Maybe a movie at my place?" He grinned. "A reprisal of the *West Side Story* nights?"

"Maybe." She angled her face, causing her shiny black hair to sweep against her porcelain cheek. Again with the shyness. "Or we could just…talk."

"Catch up."

"Yeah." A pause. "It's been a long time, Eric."

That last statement was imbued with so much unspoken promise, he couldn't catch his breath. He remembered the interrupted kiss on the stair landing, could still feel the softness of Colleen's lips, the powdery scent of her skin. He wouldn't mind a second chance at that.

Wouldn't mind it at all.

Wouldn't mind pulling Colleen into his arms and never letting her go, if you boiled it down to the bare-boned truth of the matter.

Colleen marveled over the architectural differences between her sleek high-rise condo and Eric's 1895 greystone…well, mansion, really…on a tree-lined, homey street. He was giving her the grand tour— twelve-foot ceilings, six bedrooms, eight ornate fire-places, four bathrooms, all restored to pristine period detail. She'd always been a clean-lines kind of girl, but she fell in love with the grand moldings in every room, the archways, the woodwork, the mere concept of a fully functional carriage house in the back.

"This is a lot of house for a single guy," she said.

"Believe me, I know. I could probably make do living in the carriage house alone. But I plan to stay here for a long time, maybe fill those bedrooms one day."

Colleen imagined the peal of children laughing as they pounded through all six thousand square feet of the place, the ultimate hide-and-seek utopia. She had to keep her mind off that track. She couldn't bear to think of Eric married to someone else. Couldn't bear to think of herself giving up her goals. Hence, she had to banish the whole thing from her brain. "Must take a lot to clean it."

He flipped his hands upward. "Housekeeper. Guilty as charged."

"Not to worry. I have one, too."

He planted his hands languidly on his hips and glanced around one of the front parlors. "I couldn't pass this place up once we flushed out the squatters. I got it at a steal because it was a total gut job. Tons of work, but I couldn't bear to leave a historic home like this to the house flippers. They rehab these old gals, sure. But restoring them in the way they deserve? Not always."

"Yeah." She sighed, wrapping her arms around her middle. "It's so different from my place. It feels...I don't know...like a home."

"And yours doesn't?"

She cast him a droll glance. "Mine feels like a pricey, stark, Gold Coast penthouse."

"Nothing wrong with that. A lot of people would kill to live that lifestyle."

"I know. It suits me. But this place, the whole neighborhood, it's different. In a good way."

He smiled. "Thank you. Care for some wine?"

"I'd love some."

"Follow me."

They entered a chef's dream of a kitchen, with a six-burner gas range, massive island and a butler's pantry the size of her college dorm room. "Wow. This room is totally wasted on you, take-out boy."

"You should talk."

"True. But still, wow."

He laughed, bending down to open a state-of-the-art wine chiller and extract a bottle. "You know, it came with the house." He shrugged, grabbing the opener from a nearby drawer. "I couldn't very well restore the rest of the house and leave the flecked maroon velvet wallpaper up in here."

"Flecked maroon *velvet?* In the kitchen? Tell me you have photos."

"I have an entire photo book of the restoration. I'll show it to you."

"Well, you did a great job in here." She peeked inside the oven. "No owner's manual or warranty card."

"Yeah, that was a joke, really. Occasionally my mom goes on a bend about me eating out all the time and comes over to cook for me, stocks the freezer."

"That's nice." She soaked it all in as he pulled the cork from the bottle. "A kitchen this fantastic might even inspire me to cook."

"Right," he said, punctuating it with a scoff.

She smirked. "I said, it might. Theoretically."

Wine poured, fire crackling in the living-room fireplace, lamps glowing, they settled in on opposite sides of the sumptuous sofa facing each other. She'd flipped through his photo chronology of the restoration—an amazing, and daunting, transformation—and then the intimate ambience started to freak her out. "You know," she said, setting the photo album aside, "maybe we could go over Esther's case."

His brows lifted. "You want to work?"

"It's not really work," she fibbed. "It's helping out some really deserving people. We might as well."

"Good point. I'm in." He swung his stocking feet down to the floor and retrieved the folders she'd brought him at the Lincoln Park Conservatory what seemed like years ago. "Let's start with you, since this is your work." He handed them over, then grabbed the stack of files Esther had left with him.

Through two additional glasses of wine each, Colleen pored over her research and discussed parts of them with Eric. They passed files back and forth, made notes, and somehow, of their own volition, their feet sort of tangled up together on the couch they shared.

It felt so good.

So good, so intimate, so right.

The wine had mellowed her edge enough that she felt comfortable leaving her feet where they were, playing toesies with his. In fact, she snuggled down a bit farther into the cushions and entangled herself even closer as she concentrated on a file. It was the transcript of an interview she'd done with the contractor, and she quickly became engrossed in her reading. One comment he'd let slip jumped out at her, leaving her heart pounding. She'd asked him how the construction project had gone, and he'd said "without a hitch." Exact words. Granted, they were buried in a monologue about why he was the injured party in this situation, but "without a hitch" didn't equate to triple the bill. Why hadn't she keyed on to that before? Probably worrying too much about the partners' disapproval of the pro bono case in the first place. She glanced up to find Eric studying her, the play of firelight gilding one side of his face, shadows highlighting the angles of the other.

What was he thinking?

Was the intimacy of the evening getting to him, too?

Her throat tightened. "You should read this."

"So bring it here," he drawled.

A challenge.

Feeling bold, the sensual tension pulling low and tight in her belly, she eased her legs underneath her, then scooted across the long sofa, file in hand. Close enough to smell Eric's spicy cologne, she held the file out. "Look at question fifteen. It's the part about—"

He grabbed the file and tossed it aside, leveraging her gently closer with a well-placed thigh between her legs until they were chest to chest. "We're not in law school anymore, Colleen."

She swallowed. "Indeed, no. We aren't."

"We're older now," he said, tracing the shape of her face with his gaze. "We know what we want out of life."

"Do we?"

"I do."

Unable to help herself, she reached up and ran her fingers through his hair. "And what is it you want?"

"At the moment?" Without answering, he slid her body up his until their lips were a breath apart. Her skin tingled, key parts of her anatomy throbbed.

"We shouldn't," she whispered.

"I know."

"Dangerous territory."

"True enough."

"Probably not professional."

"I don't care."

"Then, what are you waiting for?"

Eric closed the distance between them and kissed her. Not gently. Hungrily, with passion and history and the raw need for more. A deep groan in his throat rumbled through her lips as if it had come from her own body.

He wanted her.

There was no hiding that.

She pulled her mouth away and pressed herself against him, loving the way his eyes drifted closed with desire. "What are we doing?"

"We're rekindling an old friendship."

"Is that what you'd call it?"

"It's one spin we could use," he said, moving beneath her in a way that stole her breath. "And I'm also thinking of replaying the best night of my life."

She blinked. "You mean—"

"Yeah. I mean." He leaned forward and nibbled on her bottom lip. "I want to take you upstairs, Colleen. I want you in my bed. In my arms."

"Is it the wine?"

"To hell with the wine, sweetheart." He smoothed

his hand down the length of her back, cupped her rear and pulled her closer to him. "Do you feel that?"

"Yes," she whispered.

"That's all you. It's always been you."

She buried her face in his neck and slid a hand down between their bodies to caress his hardness. What could it hurt? She could handle some no-strings sex. "Now that you mention it, I didn't get a very close look at the rooms up there. I mean, there are so many."

Pushing up, he kept hold of her until they were both standing. "Six bedrooms to choose from, honey. Not to mention the bathrooms, the kitchen counters, the dining-room table. Lady's choice."

She slid her hand into his as they walked toward the stairs, and shot him an uncharacteristically shy glance. "How about that front bedroom, with the window that frames the streetlight?"

Colleen watched his face change, his expression smolder and soften all at once. "You remember the streetlight, too?" He pressed her against the wall with his body, nibbling on the side of her neck.

She let her head fall to one side. "Mmm, hmm. One side of your face was in shadow, the other glowed iridescent from that streetlight," she whispered. She smoothed her hands down the tapered muscles of his back to his waist, then tugged his shirt from his waistband and pushed it up his body. He broke away from her long enough to toss the shirt over his head, then went back to kissing her neck, her throat, nibbling on her earlobe, capturing her mouth.

"I remember it, too," he murmured against her lips, his words a vibration that radiated down her body and left her weak.

"It was one night, Eric. How could one night be so…?"

"Because it was you." He kissed her forehead. "And me." A kiss to each cheekbone. "It was right." He took her mouth once again, kissed her breathless.

Overwhelmed, Colleen pulled back for air and buried her face in his neck. "You smell the same."

"And you taste the same." Eric rested his forehead against hers. "I'm going to take you upstairs, Colleen, and make love to you until you beg me to stop. If that's not what you want, you need to tell me now."

They stared into each other's eyes for several moments, then Colleen slid her hand into his and led him silently up the stairs. She turned into the first bedroom toward the front of the house, smiled when she saw the glow of the streetlight shimmering on the bed like liquid silver. Turning to face Eric, she walked slowly backward toward the window.

Eric took a step forward.

"No," she said. "Wait."

His eyes burned with the kind of desire she hadn't experienced in years as she slowly removed her clothing, one piece at a time. She let each garment dangle from her fingertips for a moment before dropping it in a heap beside her. His fists clenched and unclenched at his sides. Her gaze never left his. The white heat of this moment, of watching him want her so badly, shook her to the core. Finally naked, she stood before him, shoulders back, head held high. She reached up and cupped her own breasts. "Do you want me as much as your eyes are saying?"

"More," he said, his voice husky.

"Why?"

"Because I've always wanted you," he said, unbuttoning his pants with the same deliberate care she'd used. She watched him with raw need pulsating through her veins, her stomach tightening at the sight of him aroused.

She lifted her gaze to his eyes.

Neither moved.

"Meet you halfway?" he suggested gently.

So sweet, so considerate. So…Eric.

He'd always made her feel like halfway wasn't nearly enough, and that was the problem. But she didn't want to succumb to fear this time. She went to him, coiled her arms around his neck and kissed him thoroughly. He lifted her off her feet and she wrapped her legs around his hips. The hot, wet warmth of her body cradled the urgent need of his. He groaned.

She moved against him, gulping.

"Coll, you feel—"

"Like I want you?"

He nodded, carrying her toward the bed. "Yes."

"I do." Her heart pounded, but the darkness emboldened her. "You know what I want?"

"Tell me."

"I want you inside me, Eric. Deep. Hard." She watched his breathing quicken. "I don't want gentle, okay? Not the first time, at least."

"The first time, huh?" Lamplight glistened off his smile as he cradled her back onto the bed, following her down to cover her with his warm body. The muscles of his chest made her breasts tingle and ache. She rubbed them against him.

He reached up to smooth his fingers down the side of her face as his body teased her below. "I've missed you."

"I can't take it, Eric. Please. I just want to feel you—" She gasped and bucked as he thrust deeply within her. Her body clenched around him, tight and slick.

"Like that?" He pulled out and slid in again, harder, deeper.

"Yes." Her fingernails dug into his shoulders, and tears stung her eyes. Eric had been the only man who'd ever broken through her tough shell to touch that vulnerable, protected place inside her. "Don't stop," she whispered, meeting his thrusts with equal fervency.

"Don't worry." He reached beneath her to cup her bottom and lift her body higher, angling to plunge deeper.

The tension in her body crested and eased, crested and eased until she reached a peak that allowed no escape except plunging over. "Eric," she gasped, her legs shaking around him. "I...I—"

"Look at me," he said. "Look into my eyes, Coll."

She did, through tears of pure pleasure, awash in a sense of home and happiness that had been missing from her life for so very long. "Eric," she moaned, letting go as they spiraled off that cliff together. Colleen wrapped herself as tightly as possible around him and closed her eyes, focusing on the sensation of him pulsating inside her, squeezing him with her own body to capture every bit of him as she rode the waves of her own climax. As they lay in a limp, tangled pile, she realized her memory hadn't played tricks on her all these years. Making love with Eric was every bit as magical as she'd remembered.

She nudged his face up until his lips met hers, kissed him long and gently. "You feel okay?"

"I feel amazing," he said.

"Yes. You do." She smiled at him in the angled silver wash of the streetlamp, shutting out the rest of the world. "But we'd better confirm that." She ran a finger slowly down his chest. "There *are* all those other rooms."

"Ah…big house. You might kill me."

"You can handle it," she teased, kissing his nose. "And, you know, you do have a gorgeous, neglected kitchen," she said, feeling his body react to the mere suggestion. "If you aren't going to actually cook in the place…"

"That's your choice?" he said, pulling away from her and offering her a hand to stand.

"For now," she said. "The night's young." Colleen felt awash in gratitude that Eric had bought such a big old house with so many rooms. By daybreak, she'd chosen them all…one after the other. Talk about a housewarming.

Chapter Nine

She'd slept with Eric Nelson.

Repeatedly.

More to the point, she'd slept with *opposing counsel*.

And, really, *slept* was a misnomer.

It should feel like a life disaster, but it didn't. She didn't seem to care. She felt too good, too satiated, too infatuated.

Eric…

Facedown on the massage table with her best friend working the knots from her upper back and neck, Colleen felt safe enough to spill her guts. Through the little open face rest on the massage table, she could only see the carpeted floor. Occasionally she'd glimpse Megan's bare feet, perfectly pedicured, as Megs curled her toes under and rolled one foot and ankle, then the other, stretching them out like a dancer.

Colleen envied Megan the fact that she was fully present in her own body at all times, even in the midst of concentration on the deep-tissue massage of Colleen's.

"I think I realized something recently," Colleen said, her voice distorted from the pressure of the cushions on her cheeks.

"What's that, hon?"

"My life sucks."

"Interesting."

"Or pathetic. Either way, I'm constantly fighting to succeed, hunting for that one achievement that will complete me, but I'm dissatisfied."

"So stop fighting," Megan said simply. "Stop hunting. Just be."

"What does that even mean?" Colleen didn't even speak Megan's language half the time.

"It depends. What do you want?"

Colleen considered that for a few moments, and her mind inevitably drifted to Eric. "I want to belong.

I want to be approachable. I want…" Why was it so hard to say it? "I might want a family, Megs. Which proves McTierney and the bunch right, I guess."

"Don't internalize their negative energy. A woman can work a high-powered career and still have a family, Coll. This is the twenty-first century."

"I know. Probably not at my firm, though."

"Aren't the men married?"

"Well, yes. That's different. To them, at least. Their 'little women' stay at home."

For a few moments, Megan was silent, as she worked along Colleen's spine with her elbows. "What's bringing about all this yearning for change in my best friend?"

Colleen sighed, squeezed her eyes shut. The only vision in her mind was the man she'd loved so thoroughly last night. "It's Eric," she said.

"Ah."

"You knew that already, didn't you?"

"Sneaking suspicion."

"He's…just so amazing, Megs. He always was, but now…it's different from law school."

"How so?"

"He's all man. Grown up and secure. We're not trying to out-do each other like we did back then."

"Didn't you graduate ahead of him?"

"A hair, yes. But now I'm thinking, what did it

matter? I alienated the only man who ever made me feel happy because of my mother's life. It didn't have anything to do with *my* life, really. And I don't think Eric would never want me to change who I am. He's like the male version of you."

"Aw, that's sweet."

"It's true. You're both so centered and calm, which pisses me off." She gave a self-deprecating laugh. "And he cares about me even though I'm a mess."

"You're not a mess. You're just you. Those of us who know you accept and love you for exactly who you are. Sounds like this Eric is one of the lucky few."

Colleen hoped Megan couldn't hear the plink-plunk of her tears on the carpeting below the massage table. "I slept with him, Megs."

Surprisingly, Megan's hands faltered, but only for a moment. "Do you mean, that night in law school?"

"No. I mean last night."

"Really?"

"Repeatedly," Colleen admitted.

"Sweetie, that's great. I've always thought of him as the one who got away for you. And you've needed a good tumble for a long time now."

"Megs!"

"Just speaking the truth. Sex is healthy for the body and the mind."

"Yes. But he and I have agreed to be just friends."

"Yet, you love him."

A beat passed. "You can tell that from the knots in my back?"

Megan laughed softly. "No, I feel it from your energy. From the tone of your voice."

Colleen groaned. "What am I supposed to do? He's opposing counsel on the biggest case of my career. I can't love him, even if I do."

"What do you want?"

"That's where it gets all jumbled up. I've worked so hard to make partner…"

"Indeed."

"But I hate my firm."

"Who wouldn't?"

"And yet, I've built my career there. I don't want to start over."

"Understandable."

"Right, but if I blow this case, I can kiss any partnership dreams goodbye."

"Why would you blow this case? Isn't it pretty much a lock? Working man versus the big bad corporation?"

"That's where things get sticky." Colleen held her breath for a second, then eased it out. She hadn't wanted to come clean with Megan, but wasn't it time to stop hiding? Stop lying? Wasn't it time to simply be herself? "There are problems with the case. I can't go into it, but—"

"Problems? What do you mean?"

"I can't say more than that. Attorney-client privilege," she said, as Megan worked her way down each leg to her supertight arches.

"It's not like I'd tell anyone."

"Not the point."

"Okay. Just answer this. Is it an ethical decision?"

"Very much so."

"Well," Megan said bluntly, "that's it, then. You can't defend anything unethical."

Colleen uttered a frustrated sound, because she'd known what Megan's stance would be. "You don't understand. I *have* to defend Jones. That's what I was hired to do. It's my duty as his attorney."

"But if it violates your code of ethics—"

"What do you think public defenders do? They represent guilty criminals their whole careers."

"Yes, but yours is a civil case. It's about a payoff."

"It's a legal gray area that's really hard to explain. I've already said more than I should. The point is, I can still win it."

"What about Eric? Does he know about this ethical dilemma, whatever it is?"

"I'm not sure."

"Have you asked him?"

"I can't do *that*. That's like showing your cards in a game of high-stakes poker." Unbidden, she recalled the night Eric's brothers were debating the World Poker Tour, and a lump rose in her throat.

"Okay, you know my stance on the whole thing, but I'm not a lawyer, thank God. And I don't know exactly what you're dealing with, double thank God. So I'll concentrate on the best friend advice angle."

"Thank you," Colleen said.

"If you win the case, what will that do to your relationship with Eric?"

"Friendship," Colleen corrected.

"Whatever it is."

"At this point, if he knows everything I do, it'll probably end it."

"Ah. Roll over, hon."

"I can't do that."

"I meant, on the massage table."

"Oh."

Megs held the sheet in a way that allowed Colleen to modestly roll to her back. Once Colleen was settled in, Megan slid a cylindrical pillow beneath her knees, then brushed the hair from Colleen's forehead. Megan grabbed her left hand and squeezed. "I'm going to assume you want my insight."

Colleen closed her eyes. "I always want your insight, you know that."

"You need to figure out what's most important, where you want to go in life, and let the rest fall away. One case victory? A partnership in a firm you despise? Or a chance with the only man you've ever loved?"

Colleen huffed. "You make it sound like such an easy choice. We're talking about my career here. And there's no guarantee the friendship would evolve beyond what it is."

"Career versus love," Megan said softly, running her thumbs down the tight muscles in Colleen's forearm.

"But I can't just throw the case. You don't understand. I'll be fired. I could be disbarred—"

"For what? Having a moral barometer?"

Colleen ignored that. "Not to mention all the life issues. I have my mortgage, my mom. I can't exactly give it all up for the greater good, now can I?"

"You hate your job. You're conflicted over the case because you have a conscience. You're in love with opposing counsel—"

"I never said that."

"You didn't have to, but okay. A friendship where you, let's see, sleep with each other, then run to your best friend and talk about wanting a family. You might not call that being in love, but—"

"I see your point."

"Anyway, I'd say, yes, you can give it all up for the greater good. The greater good for *you*."

"Is that what you think I should do? For real? As my best friend, please tell me straight-out."

"I'm not going to presume to understand the world you live and work in. That part's up to you. But I do think you should be happy, Colleen, whatever that takes. You deserve it. So find your happy place and work toward a permanent residence there."

"Got a minute?" Eric asked Jack, as they passed in the hallway.

"Sure," Jack said. "Something wrong?"

"Not at all. Just want to bring you up to speed."

Eric watched his friend perk up at the sound of those hopeful words. "Give me a moment to let my secretary know to hold my many, many, many calls."

Eric frowned. "Something up with you?"

"Imminent family crisis, as if we need that on top of everything else," Jack said ruefully.

"Is everyone okay?"

"Yes, fine. It's just that Mori Taka—Helen's new husband? Seems his daughter, Kimiko, has decided dropping out of college and returning to the nest would be a good choice for her."

"That's it?" Eric chuckled. "Things could be a whole helluva lot worse."

"You'd think. Mori's livid. Helen's in a tizzy. It's as if the poor kid is pregnant, doing drugs, getting arrested—all in one day. She's a quirky one, Kimiko. And headstrong. Anyway, enough of the family drama. Give me a sec to check in with my secretary and I'll meet you in the conference room."

"Sounds good." The two men split off in opposite directions. As Eric settled behind the table, he couldn't help but wonder if Colleen had discovered exactly the same information he had, information he was about to share with Jack Hanson. Information that proved Ned Jones cut a deal with Drake Thatcher to make bogus claims against Taka-Hanson, all for a payoff and a guaranteed job with Thatcher's company. The whole thing was another arrow slung toward Taka-Hanson from its rival. This could change everything.

Which bothered him more than it should con-sidering the explosive night he and Colleen had shared. He had a gut feeling she knew about the Jones/Thatcher deal. How could she not? She had access to one of the key players—Jones—which was a lot more than he had, and he'd been able to figure it out. Colleen was savvy and whip-smart. She had to have figured it out, too. And he'd caught the few veiled references she'd made to the case turning into a nightmare, which could only mean…she knew.

Then again, if she had gotten to the bottom of this fiasco, why hadn't she done Eric the courtesy of going to Ned Jones and convincing him to drop the fake accusations? All that intimacy, and she couldn't do the right thing? She'd still put pathetic Ned Jones ahead of Eric? Of their relationship? Had ambition truly trumped ethics in her life? The idea disheartened him. He didn't want to believe she'd make that choice. After their magical night, Eric had allowed a glimmer of hope to grow in his chest that maybe, just maybe, Colleen Delaney had changed.

Then he dug in and, with the help of a tenacious private investigator, found the ironclad connection to Thatcher.

He had financial records of payments made to Jones by Thatcher, photographs of the two of them together, even a scratchy recorded conversation during which they discussed the deal.

With this new turn of events in the Jones versus Taka-Hanson case, he wasn't so sure about Colleen's agenda anymore, and that killed him. Damn it, he was falling in love with her all over again, and he didn't want to get smacked down twice.

Moments into this disturbing train of thought, Jack entered the room, closing the door behind him. "I'm all yours. What's the good word?" He sat.

"It's not Jones." Eric refocused, leaned forward,

and tossed his old pal a stack of documents, including photographs snapped by the P.I. who did freelance work for Eric's firm. "It's Drake Thatcher's machinations. Again. He's paying Ned Jones to help take Taka-Hanson down a notch. Paying him to lie low until it's said and done, and then he'll go to work for Thatcher."

Jack stared at him in disbelief. "You're sure?"

Eric flicked a hand toward the Tyvek envelope on top. "Have a look. In addition to the photographs, I have phone records, bank records—a lot."

Jack picked it up, unwound the red string closure, extracted the stack of eight-by-tens. As he flipped through the photos of clandestine meetings between Thatcher and Jones, his complexion reddened, and he swore beneath his breath. After he'd looked at every photograph, he inhaled deeply, then blew it out. "Okay, wow. But this is good stuff."

Eric braced his elbows on the table. "A start. Guardedly good, though, Jack. Not a lock and load."

"It seems pretty clear."

"To us. But we have to convince a jury of Ned's peers, and you know how difficult that can be."

"How do we get there?"

"Ned needs to agree to roll on Thatcher."

"And the likelihood of that? Slim?"

Eric pulled a dubious expression. "To none. Problem is, there's nothing in it for Ned."

"How so?"

"He talks, his payoff is nil. And he just might wind up in prison for extortion. If he keeps his mouth shut, Colleen has enough trumped-up crap to confuse a jury and potentially win this thing. A win-win for both of them. If you were presented with that choice, being in Ned's position, what would you choose?"

Jack blinked at him a few times, taking it all in. "So we're screwed either way?"

Eric wagged his finger slowly. "Not necessarily. We've got a couple of options, both with pros and cons."

"Lay 'em on me." Jack interlocked his fingers and braced his hands behind his head.

"Option one, we take it to the judge at the hearing we have scheduled in three days. Throw it out there, good, bad and ugly."

"And the issues with that?"

Eric scrubbed his already jacked-up hair with one palm as he stood, paced. "I full-court press Colleen like that, it'll be like whacking a hornet's nest. A total betrayal—at least, that's how she'll view it. There's no way in hell she'll let her client talk if I throw her case in front of the judge without preparing her."

"Damn. You're sure?"

"Delaney's a grudge-holder and it's a huge gamble. We'd have to hope the judge rules in our favor and compels Ned Jones to talk. If the judge goes the other route—" Eric shrugged "—we're done."

Jack nodded slowly. "Option two?"

Eric leaned against the window and crossed one ankle over the other. "I've been working a pro bono case—" he rolled his hand "—soulless contractor duping a harmless group of elderly folks. A slam-dunk sympathy case, for sure, not to mention, the contractor's a dirtbag. Prior to my taking the clients on, Colleen considered doing so."

"Let me guess. Shot down by Framus and the gang?"

Eric aimed an index finger at Jack and pulled a thumb trigger.

"What a pack of jackals, those guys."

"Yeah, but Colleen really wanted to defend Esther Wellington and the others. It stung when she couldn't, so…she's been helping me a bit." Eric felt Jack's curious scrutiny, and dropped his gaze. "Providing background, and so forth."

Jack's brows rose. "Really. Huh."

Thankfully, Jack didn't probe any further. Eric sucked air through his teeth and turned his head to the side. "It's a huge risk, Jack, but she and I are actually, ah, getting along at the moment." *Understatement.* "I could lay out everything I know to her, show her the photos, try to prod her into getting Ned Jones to drop the charges."

"Mess with her conscience."

"Something like that, yes."

"Odds of success?"

Eric coughed out a humorless, monosyllabic laugh. "It's Colleen, not a parking spot. I've got no karma when it comes to her and I wouldn't bet on her even with insider tips. I don't know." He sank into his chair. "I don't expect her to break attorney-client privilege, but I can play with her conscience, bank on her feeling an obligation to talk Ned out of pursuing the charges. If I do go to her first, I'm pretty sure I won't anger her into a complete lack of cooperation." Plus he'd have a chance at a repeat of last night. "So that's something."

"Whatever you think is best, pal."

Unsettled, Eric pushed to his feet again and paced in front of the floor-to-ceiling windows, arms crossed. Jack illuminated the problem, right there. Eric wanted both to do right by his old friend *and* keep Colleen in his life, but he didn't know how, or even if, that was possible. The conflict was immense. "We've got more speed bumps down the road, regardless of what happens. Any jury we sit will have automatic sympathy for Jones. People aren't loving major corporations these days."

"Agreed." Jack hiked his chin. "And?"

Eric spun to face him. "Colleen. Again. I suspect she knows exactly what's gone down between Ned and Thatcher. If that's the case, she should've counseled her client to drop the suit already and she hasn't. We've spent…a lot of time together recently. But, other than a few veiled references that sent up my red flags, she hasn't said a word about Ned being in on the plot."

"A lot of time?"

Eric ignored that. He twisted his mouth to the side. "No matter what we do next, I'm not convinced she's going to back away from the case."

"What makes you think so?"

Eric spread his arms and huffed his skepticism. "You know her, man. She's the most ambitious woman I've ever come across. Winning will guarantee she makes partner. Backing off will guarantee she doesn't. She'll have the jury on her side, and she knows that. Plus, infuriating as it is, we have to accept that she has enough so-called evidence to give us a run for our money."

Jack leaned back, braced his hands behind his head. "Doesn't seem fair, does it?"

"It's law, Jack. It's not about fairness for firms like McTierney and the rest."

"But Colleen?" Jack squinted, baffled. "You honestly think she'd choose career advancement over integrity? Over you?"

Heat burst across his skin. "I hate to think it, but there's this niggling doubt." He laid a palm on his abs. "I can't be sure. We could offer a settlement."

Hands still locked behind his head, Jack squeezed his elbows together in front of his face and groaned. "I wish it were that easy, but we couldn't do that." He let his arms drop and implored Eric. "I hate to ask this of you, but you've got to work her, Eric. Whatever it takes. We're in deep on these new hotel projects and we're still recovering from the fiscal blow we had a few years back."

When Hanson Media and Taka merged, Eric knew.

"The company might appear flush to people outside the inner circle, but we can't take the kind of hit this case, or even a settlement, would bring. Plus, I can't do it to Robby. He's been a loyal employee far too long."

"I understand. I'll give it my all. Just know, Colleen's as savvy as they come. Driven, too. Whatever tactics I use to work her, she's going to be working me just as hard."

"If not harder."

A beat passed. He hung his head, thinking of his own integrity. "I slept with her."

"You *what?*"

Eric nodded. "It gets worse. I think I'm falling in love with her. Again."

Jack snapped his fingers. "I knew it. My hunch was correct. There was something between you in law school."

"Yeah." Eric sighed. "There was, short-lived and ultimately traumatic, but something. So you understand where I'm coming from. In a perfect world, my relationship with her would take precedence, but you hired me, and I won't let you down. Understand that. I'm in a bad spot, though. I want your honest opinion."

Jack nodded, considering. "My thoughts are, Colleen will be there when the dust settles if it's really meant to be for you two. But we're definitely behind the eight ball, pal," Jack said, grimacing with regret. "I don't see any other option than to chalk up and go for the corner pocket."

Eric's gut sank, but he nodded once. "Then that's what we'll do."

Chapter Ten

Colleen took Megan's words to heart, really searched her soul. Before she could even consider the personal complications Eric brought to the mix, she knew it was time to come clean about Ned Jones to someone at her firm. Certainly her own prospects for partnership were in jeopardy, but it had ballooned far beyond that. This case could impact everyone. As infuriating as the old boys' club could be, *she,* at least, had a conscience, and didn't feel right about blindsiding them. The question remained, who was the lesser of the evils she should talk to?

McTierney and Framus were automatically out. As the oldest two and the least accepting of her gender, she could feel their patronizing disdain for her, like oil on the skin, every time the three of them shared airspace. Wenzel was a bit of a spineless weasel. Though she got along with him well enough one-on-one, he'd never go against Frick and Frack. She couldn't risk pulling him into her confidence. That left Harrison Scott, the newest partner in the firm. Although older than her by at least a decade, Harrison was closest to her in age. But she had to remember he was a company man just like the rest of them. She needed to keep her wits about her, no matter what.

She scheduled an early morning coffee appointment with him at The Chambers. Wearing her most conservative, slate-colored wool suit and carrying all she'd dug up about Ned and his involvement with Thatcher—including the taped interview with Ned during which he spilled all—she headed to the restaurant. Trepidation danced in frenzied spins and lifts in her stomach, and food was the last thing on her mind. But she knew meeting Harrison off-site was the only viable option. So coffee. The ultimate non-reason for people to get together.

She raised a hand to signal him when he entered the restaurant. He responded with a terse nod and headed her way, his steps strong and measured. Heavy.

"Thanks for meeting me," Colleen said after he sat across from her in the same back booth she and Eric had occupied less than two weeks earlier.

"Sure," he said brusquely, slipping the wool scarf from his neck and shrugging out of his overcoat. "I don't have a lot of time—"

"Of course. If we can just order coffee."

Harrison Scott crossed his arms on the edge of the table. "That's fine."

Colleen gestured to their waitress, set the menus aside, then dove in. Really, was there any easier way? "I need to bring this issue to someone at the firm, but I don't want to cause an uproar if it's not necessary. I'd like another opinion, though."

"Okay. So here I am. Lay it on me," Harrison said, checking his watch as if she wouldn't notice the insulting gesture. As if meeting with his own colleague was an annoying time suck he couldn't fit in to his oh-so-important schedule.

The waitress scooped up their menus and clunked a thick mug of coffee before each of them. "Anything else, folks?"

"No," Colleen said. "Thanks."

Steam and tension swirled into the air between her and Harrison Scott. She cleared her throat, glanced around at the occupants of the nearby tables, then spoke in a lowered tone. The place burst with lawyers. One never knew who might overhear. "It's about the Ned Jones case."

"I figured. It's the only big case you have."

Ouch. She ignored that. She worked a more than full caseload, not that she received credit for it. "We could have a nightmare on our hands."

Harrison, prematurely gray but young in the face, frowned with concern. "Can you elaborate?"

Rather than explain the entire fiasco, Colleen extracted a mini-digital recorder from her handbag and slid it toward him. When he didn't move, she pushed the play button herself and had the questionable "joy" of reliving whiny Ned Jones laying bare the tangled web of deceit into which he'd pulled her and the entire firm. His confession of the deal he'd struck with Thatcher: to accuse and discredit Robby Axelrod and Taka-Hanson, all for a payoff and a job with Thatcher's company. She'd recorded Ned's admission that the whole case was a lie, a setup.

When the interview ended, both she and Harrison remained quiet amidst the bustle and chatter around them.

Harrison didn't move.

Colleen watched him.

Finally, she reached over and palmed the recorder. She slipped it back in her bag, then tossed her hair and raised her eyebrows at him. "Is that elaboration enough?"

"Yes. But what's the problem?" Harrison asked.

Her hands went tingly as she realized Harrison Scott was not on her side. "What do you mean, what's the problem? It's all a lie. The case is based on lies."

Harrison half-laughed, shaking his head. "Colleen. You've been a lawyer long enough to know that doesn't matter."

"But—"

He widened his eyes, a belligerent expression on his face. "No buts. Do you have enough circumstantial evidence to plant doubt in a jury's collective, and might I add, simple mind?"

Wow, she hadn't realized how jaded Harrison Scott had become. He was a different man from the one she'd known before he'd leapfrogged her into a partner position. "Well, I think so, but—"

"Then—" he spread his arms "—win the damn case. What's the issue?"

Frozen, she blinked at him. Harrison wasn't the confidant she hoped he'd be. He wasn't anything she hoped he'd be. Why did that constantly surprise her with the guys in her office?

Stupid. Stupid, stupid, stupid.

"Does it bother you at all, Harrison, that we may

well destroy a man's career when he doesn't deserve it? That Taka-Hanson will be paying a massive price for a trumped-up charge?"

His facial expression didn't change.

"Okay," Colleen said, on an exhalation. "I'll take that as a no." The waitress approached with the carafe for refills, but Colleen held up a palm to ward her off. She couldn't stomach another drop and didn't really care, at this point, if Harrison wanted a warmer.

Once the waitress retreated, Harrison leaned in. "Listen carefully. You don't work for Taka-Hanson."

"I'm well aware of that, thank you." Ice crackled off her words.

"Then let me give you a bit of friendly advice if you ever plan on making partner at this firm. Win. Whatever case is handed to you, win the damn thing. Pure and simple, that's what they want. That's what I want. That's what you should want. Any attorney worth his weight can grasp that simple concept."

Worth his *weight.* She held steady even though the pointed sexist barb stung. They came so frequently, she'd learned to deflect them as much as possible, but she'd been feeling raw lately, and this one pierced her shield. Or maybe she'd dropped her shield altogether.

Who knew anymore?

The only thing she knew was that she'd made a grave misstep talking about the case to Harrison or any of the partners. She had no doubt Harrison would scurry back to the firm and inform everyone else about their little meeting. Even if she won this case now, her job might be in jeopardy. Beneath the table, she gripped her thighs with her hands until her fingernails stung the skin beneath the wool fabric.

She'd never felt so alone in her life.

Wrong versus right? Truth versus lies? Unclear.

Eric Nelson was a man and an excellent attorney, yet his goal wasn't to *win* regardless of the facts of any given case. His goal was justice.

Did that make him wrong?

Or had she been wrong all along, and Eric was right?

Carefully controlling her tone, she said, "I'm not saying I don't want to win the case, Harrison, or that I won't, but—"

"I said, no buts," Harrison said. He flicked a glance at his watch again, then impaled her with a flinty stare. "Let me put it to you this way. Win the Jones case, or your career with the firm is over." He stood.

Everything inside her tilted on its axis and her skin flashed over with raging heat. She swallowed past a throb that had begun in the side of her neck. "Is that a threat?" she asked, softly.

"I'm the junior partner," he said, with a scoff, as he stuffed his arms into his overcoat. "I don't have the ability to threaten."

"And yet, you said the words."

He didn't meet her gaze as he knotted the plaid scarf. "It's just what I've heard around the office."

Her body went from hot to flash frozen in an instant. "They're testing me? Did they know Ned Jones was full of crap when they begrudgingly *handed* me the case?"

"You're still not getting it." Harrison braced his hands on the edge of the table and leaned in. "It doesn't matter whether they are or not, whether they knew or not, if you win the damn case, does it? You wanted another opinion? I'd suggest you stop fretting and focus on that." He chucked a five-dollar bill on the table to cover his coffee, nodded to her once, and left.

Colleen couldn't move. Couldn't breathe. Her entire law career seemed to zip before her eyes on fast-forward.

Fretting.

Would he have accused a male attorney of fretting?

When the bell over the door jangled Harrison's exit, Colleen released a whoosh of air. The restaurant had filled up, but the cacophony of voices melted into one, unintelligible buzz in her brain. She rested her forehead in her fingertips, elbows braced on the table edge.

Things had gone horribly wrong.

Once upon a time, she knew right from wrong, believed in those simple concepts. But she'd lost touch with them along the way.

How had that happened? When had it happened? And why?

Long ago, she may have thought winning all her cases fell under the category heading of *right,* but with the Jones situation? She wasn't so sure. Harrison had been correct about one thing. If she didn't win, her career at the firm was over. What she couldn't figure out was whether or not that was such a bad thing.

Or was a reconnection and one night of great sex with Eric once again distorting her grand plan, an eerie repeat of law school? She didn't even know how Eric felt about her, really. He wanted to win the case, too…

Plus, she had her mortgage, her mother, her mental state. She had to think of herself, and that meant keeping her job, even if she despised it.

Right?

Robby Axelrod, the beleaguered Taka-Hanson employee who was nothing but a pawn in their game, popped into her mind and brought along a poison dart of guilt. Did he have a mortgage? A family? Children? What was his mental state at this point? Was she being selfish thinking only of herself?

Confusion, indecision and the overwhelming aroma of frying bacon nearly suffocated her. All she could think of was escape. She scrambled to her feet and dug through her purse for some cash for the coffee.

Her life felt perilously out of control, distended, on the verge of bursting. Something had to give. She'd tried talking to Harrison. Failure.

She had no other choice now but to talk to Eric.

Before she took that critical step, however, she needed some sort of a plan.

Eric was deeply immersed in preparatory work for the upcoming Jones versus Taka-Hanson hearing when his secretary, Jennifer, did her signature *tap-tap, tap-tap* on the door.

He glanced at the darkness beyond his windows, then frowned up at the clock on the front of one of the antique scales he collected and displayed in specially built shelves along one wall of his office. They reminded him of what he valued in life: balance.

Speaking of balance, shouldn't Jennifer have gone home by now? It was late. He might be a little into the workaholic mode at the moment, but that didn't mean his employees needed to follow suit. "Come in."

Jennifer peeped her head around the cherrywood door. "Someone here to see you if you're not busy."

He stifled a sigh. He'd never taken his frustration out on any of his secretaries and he didn't plan to start now, with the best of the bunch. "I am busy. Who is it?"

"Colleen Delaney."

Desire bloomed inside him. Along with surprise. And the effervescence of joy. He blinked. "Colleen?"

"Yeah."

"Here?"

Jennifer made an effort to hide a smile. "Yep."

"I'm sorry, I just wasn't expecting… Never mind. Send her in, thanks. And, hey. Jen, you don't have to work late just because I am."

"I know. I just wanted to be here in case you needed anything," she said. "I don't mind. It's a big case."

Note to self: give Jen a whopping bonus or put her in for a raise in the near future. She was a dream secretary, and he didn't want to lose her. For now, he settled on a smile. "I appreciate the team play, but put in for overtime, then feel free to head out."

"You sure? I could brew you a pot of coffee before I leave if you're going to be a while."

"Thank you, but I can make my own coffee. You're young. Go have fun in the city."

Jennifer grinned. "Okay, thanks. I'll send Ms. Delaney right in."

Eric thought about putting his tie back on, rolling down his crumpled shirtsleeves. Attempting to tame his unruly hair. But, then again, why? Business hours had long since passed and Colleen had seen him in a lot less. Recently. Surely she wouldn't care about his work-rumpled appearance.

His body tightened with the memory of their night together, but he shoved it out of his mind. He'd bet she hadn't popped by for an instant replay.

He regretted his decision to remain so disheveled when she entered the room. She wore some kind of deceptively simple, slinky black dress that crossed over her delectable body and tied at the waist. A peep of red silk and lace showed at the deep V between her breasts, and shiny, metallic high heels turned her calves into works of art.

"Wow," he said, standing up and moving around his desk to the more casual seating area. "You look incredible, Colleen. Hot date?"

"Ha, ha."

He gestured to the small sofa. "Make yourself at home. To what do I owe the honor of this unexpected visit?"

She took a seat on the sofa and crossed her legs, exposing more of their toned length to his appreciative gaze in the process. "Thank you. I was in the neighborhood. Actually—" long sigh "—I needed to see a friendly face. Hope that's okay."

"Of course." He sat on the other end of the sofa, badly wanting to kiss her. He didn't think she'd be open to the idea of that here in the office, though. "Let me guess. Crappy day at Framus and Friends?"

"Something like that." She glanced around. "Nice digs, Nelson. They must like you here."

He made a mental note of the slight bite to her words, but moved on. It didn't seem to be directed at him, and she didn't seem ready to talk about it. Taking in the space around him with fresh eyes, he had to admit, his expansive corner office with two walls of windows looking out over the Chicago skyline did tend to impress. Especially now, when darkness fell and a zillion lights in the city twinkled like a diamond-studded blanket. "Thanks. I do okay." He caught her looking at his antique scales collection. "Like them?"

"They're lovely." She shook her head slowly, then cocked her head and regarded him. "You're a constant surprise. I never would've pegged you for a collector."

"I'm really not."

She hiked one eyebrow.

"In general, I mean. Those serve as a reminder of why I got into this field in the first place." He smiled. "Especially on bad days like the one you seemed to have had." A beat passed. "Want to talk about it?"

"No. Well, sort of, but…" Colleen's gaze moved uncertainly over the mounds of paper on his desk, and something in her expression shifted. "No," she said firmly. "I should've called first. I don't want to interrupt. You seem busy." She shouldered her handbag, as if to leave.

"And you seem unsettled." He slid closer.

"That obvious, huh?"

He nodded. "Plus, I'm never too busy for you, and you're my favorite interruption." He took a chance and reached out for one of her hands, running his thumb across the knuckles.

"What are we doing, Eric?" she whispered, her voice shaky. "What is this?"

"Coll, come on. Tell me what you need. An ear? A shoulder? A drink?" *An hour or two in my bed?*

"If only a drink could solve anything." She laughed, without mirth. "I'd actually hoped you'd be free for dinner. Impulsive, I know."

"Dinner?" he asked, like an idiot.

The corner of her mouth quivered up. "Strangely, yes. Dinner is what people do around this time of day. It's one of the three widely recognized meals."

"Witty." He shook his finger at her. "Very witty."

"So what do you say? I know I barged in on you, probably at a bad time, but will you have dinner with me?"

"I'd like nothing more," he said, then spread his arms wide and glanced down at himself. "Although, I'm not dressed to the nines like you. Sadly, I'm not even dressed to the fours or fives, so you'll have to give me time to stop home and change."

"Whatever works." She stood. "I should take something home to Mom, anyway. I haven't been shopping lately and I can't very well starve the woman."

"Sounds like we have a plan. I can pick you up."

"Okay. I seem to remember the promise of a visit to the Bourgeois Pig Cafe that never came to fruition." She peered down at her attire uncertainly. "If I'm not *over*dressed—"

"Trust me, sweetheart," Eric said, as he stood and retrieved his jacket. "No one with eyes and a brain would ever complain about that dress, no matter where you went." He crossed to her and lifted her chin with one finger, touching his lips to hers once, twice, the third time a little deeper.

That undeniable chemistry swirled and bubbled between them, just as it always had. He couldn't help but stir the pot. He pulled her closer, kissed her deeper as he smoothed his hands down the curves of her body. He wanted her, no doubt about it. Right here, right now.

She swayed into him, falling into the kiss for a moment, then pulled away with a moan of what he hoped was regret. "We can't do this, Eric."

"It's okay," he whispered. "Everyone's gone."

"I know, but—"

"I understand." He smoothed the back of his fingers down her silky cheek, then let his hand drop. "Give me a sec to power down my computer, turn off my Christmas tree lights and we're out of here."

"Christmas tree?"

He pointed toward a massive potted jade plant at the apex of the two windows. He'd draped it with white twinkle lights.

"Aw, that's so cute, Nelson. You're like the human version of a suburban shopping mall, decorating for Christmas before Thanksgiving."

"It's festive," he said defensively, but with a wink, as he pulled the plug. "You can take the boy out of the burbs, but apparently you can't take the burbs out of the boy. Anyway, it makes the plant feel special."

"I see," she said dubiously. "Did the plant tell you that?"

"Mock away, Delaney, but plants give off a vibe."

"I'll have to take your word for it."

"Don't you have plants?" *Didn't everyone?*

Vulnerability showed in her eyes. "No, I guess I don't. We moved around too much when I was growing up to keep living things. And now, I don't have time or energy to keep anything but myself alive," she said.

He ignored the pang of pity in his middle, knowing she wouldn't appreciate it. He decided to keep things light. "I don't know," he drawled, draping his arm over her shoulder and leading her toward the door. "Looking like that, I'd say you could bring the dead back to life."

They left the office with Colleen laughing.

A small victory, in Eric's book.

Chapter Eleven

They'd made plans for Eric to pick her up in front of her building in forty-five minutes. Colleen picked up Thai food for her mom and headed home, only to find Moira asleep—still. And she'd been asleep earlier in the day, too. Colleen seriously worried her mother might be spiraling deeper into depression, but she didn't know what to do about it.

She stowed the takeout in the woefully empty refrigerator, left a note for her mom on the counter, and flicked on a hall light. After brushing her teeth and refreshing her lipstick, she killed time by glancing around her condo, scrutinizing it as a newcomer or a potential buyer might.

Tasteful.

Impeccably clean and organized.

Sterile.

Eric was right. The place needed plants. And, considering how much she loved the Lincoln Park Conservatory, how alive she felt walking through the gardens, it seemed ludicrous that she'd never thought to bring some of that serenity into her own environment. All it took was a little jade plant festooned with Christmas lights to remind her how much her life was lacking.

Greenery.

And a man like Eric.

You can't have everything, Colleen.

Right.

She made a mental note to buy greenery, and as she did so, she thought perhaps a trip to the nursery might inspire Mom to leave the condo. Then again…did her mom even like plants? She didn't know, and that made her feel hollow and teary. It was as if two polite strangers shared the condo.

Colleen checked the clock on her coffeemaker, paced, stared out the windows. It had begun to snow again. She sat and flipped through a magazine, but it couldn't keep her attention. With a sigh, she tossed it aside and checked her cell phone. It had been an hour. Had Eric changed his mind about dinner?

As if reading her thoughts, her cell phone rang.

"Eric?"

"Hey. Sorry I'm late."

"I was beginning to worry." She grabbed her coat. "I'll be right down."

"Actually, a little…problem cropped up."

"Are you okay?"

"I'm fine, but—"

"You're not downstairs."

"No, I'm downstairs. Listen, can I come up for a few minutes?"

Colleen glanced nervously at her mother's bedroom, but why? There wasn't a reason in the world Colleen couldn't have a colleague stop by the house. Except she'd somehow stopped thinking of Eric as a colleague right about the third time she'd gasped out his name in bed the other night. Mom would pick up on that vibe, and the thought of that happening turned her stomach. Thank God she was asleep. "Of course," Colleen said. "Tell Joaquin—the doorman—you're here to visit me. He'll call up to confirm."

"Will do."

As she waited for Eric to make it up to her floor, Murphy's Law kicked in, and Mom emerged from her room in a pair of aqua satin pajamas, rubbing the sleep from her eyes and limping.

Colleen rose from the sofa and crossed to her. "Why are you limping?"

"Oh, it's nothing. I slipped earlier getting out of the shower. But it's fine."

"Okay," Colleen said uncertainly, linking the fingers of both hands and squeezing on the knot of her fists. "Do you need to see the doctor?"

"I have an appointment for tomorrow."

Colleen gulped, irrationally guilty that her mom had slipped and she hadn't been around to help. "I bought you pad Thai. It's in the fridge."

"Thank you, sweet pea. I think I'll put on some water for tea."

Colleen's heart began to thud. This shouldn't be so difficult. She cleared her throat. "I, uh, have a colleague stopping by for a few minutes. We have a business dinner."

Mom swiveled to face her, panicked. Moira Delaney never saw visitors without being fully pulled together, from the hair to the makeup to the outfit. "Here?"

"No. We're going out. He's just picking me up." Colleen braced herself.

As expected, Moira's face brightened at the mere mention that the colleague in question was male, and she smoothed her hair. "How lovely. I'll just go put on a robe. Do you mind setting the kettle to boil?"

"Not at all."

The women went about their tasks, and moments later, the doorbell chimed. Colleen hurried to open it.

Just seeing Eric's face calmed her.

Which made her seem a lot like her mother….

Something in her chest twisted.

She released a breath. "Come on in." Eric seemed to be holding his coat strangely. "Are you sure you're not injured? Were you in an accident?"

"Near miss," Eric said, as he crossed the threshold and soaked in the surroundings.

"Oh, my gosh, what happened?"

"Promise you won't be angry."

She spun to face him. "Have you been drinking?"

"Ah, no. It was this little guy." A scruffy, adorable puppy popped his head out of Eric's coat and thumped his tail against Eric's torso. White and butterscotch colored, with longish floppy ears. "He was in the road. I almost hit him."

"Oh, no!"

"Yeah. So I stopped and picked him up. Asked around a bit, but nobody seemed to know who he belonged to. I'm sorry for bringing him into your—

wow—your beautiful condo straight out of the pages of *Architectural Digest.*"

"Thanks."

"But I couldn't leave him out there. It's snowing, and—"

"N-no. Of course you couldn't." A puppy. She'd never had a puppy. She didn't exactly know what to do. "So, okay. Should you…set him down?"

Eric cringed, squatting down to set the bundle of wild fur on the floor. "He and I just met. I don't know the extent of his house-training."

"Oh. Well, travertine is easy to clean."

Just then, Moira emerged from her bedroom, looking lovely in a long, jade robe and lipstick, but Colleen took note of the hollows in her mom's cheeks, the darkness beneath her eyes.

"Hello there," Moira said, her gaze on Eric.

He stood. "Hello. You must be Mrs. Delaney."

"Eric," Colleen said. "My mom, Moira. Mom, this is Eric Nelson."

Moira limped closer, extending her tiny hand. "It's a pleasure to—"

"Yap! Yap!"

Everyone glanced down at the puppy, and Moira gasped. "Oh, my! It's a little Cavalier King Charles Spaniel." Favoring her good knee, Moira eased her way down onto the floor and patted her lap, urging the puppy closer. He bounced over to her and she scooped him up, burying her face in his fur.

Eric glanced at Colleen questioningly. She shrugged.

"He's adorable, Eric," Moira said. "What's his name?"

"He's not mine, actually."

"He was wandering in the street and Eric almost hit him," Colleen added, shaking the confusion from her head. "Mom, how did you know his breed?"

Moira held the puppy out in front of her and kissed him on the forehead. "Animal Planet," she said. "One of those dog shows. Isn't he just an angel?"

The teakettle whistled, and Colleen hurried from the room to remove it from the burner. When she re-entered, Eric was sitting cross-legged on the floor with her mother, both of them playing with the puppy. It was the first time she'd seen her mother animated since the surfing accident and subsequent breakup with boyfriend number God-only-knew.

Moira glanced up. "Sweet pea, can we keep him?"

Colleen felt an odd sense of role reversal that creeped her out. "Mom, I don't know. In a high-rise?"

"He won't get very big. He's a tiny breed."

"Yes, but he'll need to go out—"

"I can take him outside," Moira said. "I don't have anything else to do."

The lightbulb went off in Colleen's head, but she wanted to downplay her excitement. She stooped over and rubbed the little puppy's chin. "You'll be able to walk him? Because he'll need that, and I'll be at work—"

"I'd love to walk him." Moira cradled him against her chest again.

"Really?"

"Gosh, what should we name him?"

"No, no, no." Colleen crisscrossed her hands. "Don't name him yet. He might belong to someone, and that'll make it harder to give him back."

"He didn't have tags." Moira glanced at Eric. "Did he? Or a collar?"

"No, he didn't."

"But he might have a microchip," Colleen said. Her mom's light expression dimmed a bit, so she added, "I'll take him to the vet tomorrow and have him scanned." She gulped. "If he doesn't have a microchip, we can keep him. Unless—Eric, did you plan on keeping him?"

Eric shook his head. "He'd be alone all day. That wouldn't be fair to the little guy."

"Exactly. Chip and I can spend our days together, just the two of us, right baby?" Moira cooed, laughing when the puppy nibbled on her nose.

Colleen smiled. "You're calling him Chip?"

Moira hiked a shoulder. "It's a chip that will determine if he can stay or not. I think it suits him."

Eric laughed.

"You kids go on to dinner. Chip and I will be fine here together."

"Well, let us get you set up first, Mom." Colleen tapped her chin with an index finger. "Let's see…you'll need…" She had no idea what he'd need.

She'd never had a pet. Not a pet, not a plant, not a single living thing for which she was responsible. And she had the audacity to think about family? Her fists tightened by her side. Who did she think she was?

"Do you have a big box anywhere?" Eric asked, sliding his palms together slowly. "And an old blanket?"

"Yes. Great. Good thoughts." She'd gotten a delivery yesterday and hadn't yet taken the crate to the incinerator. "I'll just get that and—"

"Were you about to make tea, Moira?" Eric asked. "I can do that for you."

"How sweet of you. Yes."

He stood and met Colleen's glance with a wink. She'd never loved anyone so much as right that moment, so much that she knew it would never, ever happen.

After they'd set up a makeshift bed and water bowl for Chip in Moira's room and served Mom tea and pad Thai on the bed tray, Eric and Colleen left, promising to bring home dog food and other supplies.

The elevator doors whooshed shut, and Colleen pressed Eric against the wall, saying everything with her lips that she hadn't been able to say out loud. When the ding signaled the lobby floor, she pulled away.

"Wow. What was that for?"

"For you being amazing."

"Because I almost hit a dog?"

She smiled, curling her arm around the crook of his elbow as they nodded to Joaquin at the doorman's desk and headed out. "No, because you accomplished, in five minutes, what I haven't been able to accomplish in over a year. You made Mom smile and got her to agree to leave the house."

Playfully, Eric stood up straighter and tugged at his lapels. "I did all that? Damn, I'm good."

"You are," Colleen said. *Too good for me.* "In so many ways, I might add."

Eric stopped, turned to her. He ran his hands into the sides of her hair and tipped her face up. "What are you trying to say?"

Her heart felt huge in her chest, her connection

to this man overwhelming. "I'm saying…I'm not hungry. At least, not for food." Despite warning bells clanging in her skull, she reached up and kissed him. "Let's go to your house."

Two hours later, on the crest of her third climax, Colleen cried out and then simply…cried. She broke down and couldn't hold back the regret. For time wasted, for her current dilemma, for her deep, impossible love of this man. Not only did her career, her home, her mom's care and her self-esteem hang in the balance, now she had a dog.

A dog.

Another mouth to feed. That tipped the scales.

She hated crying. But she couldn't stop. It was as if she'd needed to cry since losing Eric in law school, only she hadn't seen it until now, when she was about to lose him again. She covered her face with both hands.

"Hey, now." Eric rolled to his back and pulled her on top of him.

She buried her face in his neck, inhaling his scent, committing it to memory.

"What's wrong? Did I hurt you?"

"No, of course not." She gulped. "I'm sorry. So, so sorry."

He smoothed her hair with one hand, held her

tightly against his chest with the other. "Sweetheart, talk to me. What do you have to be sorry about?"

"You make me feel so alive."

He reached for a tissue, handed it to her. "And that makes you sad?"

"That I've moved through life like the walking dead? That I've made difficult decisions and still have to?" She wiped her eyes and sniffed. "Yeah. A little sad. I just wanted my life to turn out differently from hers."

"What are we talking about here? Whose life?" He scooted up to a half-sitting position against the headboard.

Colleen sat up next to him, clutching a pillow to cover her nakedness. "My mom's." She twisted her mouth to the side.

"Was her life so bad?"

"From the perspective of her daughter? Yes." She peered at Eric through wet lashes. He waited for her to talk, and she found that she wanted to. Needed to. She couldn't cut him off at the knees, and the hearing was only two days away. "I never knew my dad. But so what, you know? Mom and I could've had a great life together alone, if only that had been enough for her."

"It wasn't?"

She shook her head. "She went from man to man, desperate for someone to take care of her. Half the time she forgot that she needed to take care of me. She'd completely change her life for these guys, to try to meet some ideal that was forever out of reach." Colleen shook her head. "I can't even count the number of times she got her heart broken, how often we moved, how many 'dads' I had or schools I attended. All because she had that single-minded goal in mind of being a wife, no matter what it did to her world or to mine. It disgusted me."

"But you're not like that, Colleen."

"I am, Eric. That's what I'm trying to tell you."

"How so?"

Heart shattering, she reached out and smoothed her palm over his beard stubble. "Because all I've ever wanted was to make partner in a major law firm. And, okay, I may have picked the wrong law firm, but it's too late now. Anything less feels like failure."

A wariness slid into his expression. "Meaning?"

She hiccupped. "I can win the case, I *have* to win it—"

He grabbed her wrist. "Colleen, wait—"

She pulled away gently, then stood, distancing herself physically, mentally, emotionally. "As much as I'm falling in love with you, Eric Nelson, as much as it kills me to do this, I can't destroy my career for a man. Not even you. Because then I'll be just like her."

Panicked now, somehow numb despite the searing pain, she stumbled through getting dressed. She had to get out from under the weight of his disapproval, the crush of her own devastation. Megan told her to chase happiness, but she was doing just the opposite, and she couldn't make herself stop. Fear had a choke hold on her.

Why wasn't he yelling at her?

That would make things so much easier.

"So that's it, then?" he said instead. His voice calm. Steady. "We have amazing sex, you drop the bomb that you're falling in love with me but screwing me over anyway, I take you home, case closed?" He reached for the lamp.

"Don't," she said, softening it with, "please." He hesitated, then dropped his hand to the bedsheets covering his lower half. "You don't have to—I'll call a cab."

"You're actually going to do this to me twice, Coll?"

Tears ran anew down her cheeks. "I can't walk away from the case, Eric." She slipped her feet clumsily into her shoes. "Try to understand—"

"Oh, I understand."

He said it so calmly, she couldn't read him. And she couldn't make out his features in the moonlit room, which was probably for the best. "You do?" A flicker of hope.

"I understand that you haven't changed as much as I thought you had."

His words cut, twisted. She couldn't take a breath. "I'm sorry," she gasped, heading toward safety.

"You know what the saddest part about this whole thing is?" he asked, stopping her in the doorway with his tone.

She hung her head.

Waited.

Didn't trust herself to speak.

"It's just a case, Coll. An empty, meaningless lawsuit that you're forming your entire life around based on some fears from childhood." A beat passed. "And, incidentally, I'm in love with you, too. Stupid me, huh?"

Chapter Twelve

Colleen called in to the office the next morning and told the secretary she shared with junior attorneys that she'd be working from home. Which wasn't exactly true. She'd made herself a pot of coffee and climbed back in bed, alternating between dozing and crying and feeling like she'd suffered a death. She'd just grabbed the remote and begun channel surfing when a knock sounded on her door.

"Come in," she said, eyes fixed on the television without really caring what was on the screen.

Mom came in, dressed, smiling and not limping

quite as much. Chip bopped in beside her, his little rear end getting in front of him sometimes. "Hey, puppy," Colleen said, dangling her hand off the end of the bed for the little dog to sniff. "Were you a good boy last night?" Her chin quivered. The darn little dog reminded her of Eric and probably always would.

Moira said, "He was perfect. He's a wonderful puppy."

Colleen's tummy wrung out with something that felt strangely like jealousy. "I wish I'd been 'a wonderful puppy,'" she said, in an unwarranted biting tone.

"Excuse me?" Moira cocked her head curiously.

"Never mind. I'm rambling." She couldn't take this one out on her mom, just because Moira seemed more alive around a little dog than around her own daughter. Colleen hadn't exactly left the door open for mother-daughter closeness. Besides, this wasn't about Chip. Or Mom. It was about Eric, and Colleen had made the decision to walk away from him all on her own. None of that keen self-insight made her feel any better, though.

She ran her fingers through her hair and settled back against her pillows, overwhelmed with all she had to do. She wanted to stay in bed all day. "What time do I need to drive you to the doctor's office?"

"No need. I've had Joaquin arrange a cab. I knew you'd be working," Mom said pointedly.

"Okay." Colleen watched Chip sniff a small throw pillow she'd tossed off the side of the bed, then curl up on it. "I'll take him to the vet day after tomorrow to get scanned for a microchip, okay? Tomorrow I have the hearing, and today…" She shook her head as her eyes misted over.

"I can take him. There's a vet's office right next to Dr. Flynn's building. I've already called and they can work me in before my own appointment, then they'll keep Chip until I'm finished."

"So you're just going to take him without me?" Colleen asked, in a watery tone.

Moira sat on the edge of the bed and laid one hand atop Colleen's. "Are you okay, sweet pea?"

"I'm not feeling well, Mom. That's all."

"Can I get you anything?"

"No, thanks." All she needed was Eric, and she couldn't have him and her life, too. "How's your knee?"

"It's fine. I've walked Chip twice today without any problems." Moira pressed her lips together, measuring. "Why won't you talk to me about this?"

"Because, Mom!" Damn it, Colleen thought. Damn tears.

"Does your…feeling ill have anything to do with your friend, Eric Nelson?"

Colleen jutted her chin out stubbornly, then thought *screw it*. Hadn't she always wanted the kind of mother-daughter relationship where they could confide in each other? "Mom, were you ever in love? I mean, truly in love?"

Moira let her shoulders rise and fall on a sigh, then stared off in the distance. "Once."

"Once? Then why did you keep dating, falling for all those guys?"

Mom squeezed her hand. "I don't know. I realize what my crazy dating life did to you, Colleen. But I was young and stupid. Heartbroken."

That was the closest she'd ever come to an apology. "So who was the guy?"

Moira rubbed her thumb over the back of Colleen's hand for several moments. "Your father."

What? "But then, why didn't you marry him?"

"He was…already married."

Colleen squeezed her eyes shut. She should've known. "Why, Mom?"

"Because falling in love doesn't always happen with the person who's most convenient, the most problem-free. Life is messy, sweet pea. You can't control everything."

"Did he love you?"

"Yes."

"Did he love me?" Her voice cracked.

"I never told him about you."

"What? Why not?"

"He wasn't going to leave his wife. I knew that. And I didn't want to force him to choose and ending up resenting both of us."

Colleen slipped her hand out from under her mom's and covered her face with both palms. "Would he have chosen us?"

"I think so. Because of you."

Colleen peered questioningly at her mom, as visions of a Nelson-like upbringing swirled in her head, a swarm of what-could've-been bees.

"His wife wasn't able to have children, so I think, yes. He might've divorced her and married me." She shrugged. "But I couldn't do that to her."

"Yet, you could sleep with her husband."

"I never claimed to be perfect," Moira said, leveling her with a stare. "And this happened a long time ago. I like to think I've finally learned my lesson in that regard. I never wanted you to feel second best."

Colleen scooted up, spread her arms. "But I did feel second best. My whole life."

"I'm sorry," Moira whispered, her chin quivering. "I never intended to be…a terrible mother."

Guilt stabbed Colleen. "You weren't terrible."

"I made you feel second best. Look that up in the dictionary of motherhood. It'll be under the word terrible." A tear spilled over, and she sniffed and wiped it away.

Colleen opened her arms. "I didn't mean to make you cry, Mom." The two women embraced.

"You're just like him, Colleen. You may look like me, but in personality? Hands down."

"Really?"

"Yes. I've always admired that fire in you. The drive. Your independence."

Colleen laid her cheek on her mother's small shoulder. "But I'm unhappy."

"I know, sweet pea."

"What should I do about it?"

"You can meet your father if you want to."

Colleen's heart lurched. For a moment, she considered it, but what purpose would it serve? To disrupt his life, throw this on his wife, after thirty-four years? "No. You're the only parent I need. That won't help anything. Any other ideas?"

Moira kissed her on the cheek, then pulled apart and implored her, "I made you feel second best, and I'll have to live with that the rest of my life. Don't follow in my footsteps. Put yourself first, sweet pea. For once. Before it's too late."

That's the part her mom didn't realize. It was

already too late. Her own tears reappeared, and she let them flow. "We need plants in this house."

Moira blinked. "What?"

"Plants. Greenery. Living things." She sniffed. "Will you go shopping for them with me next week?"

"Of course, I'd love to." Moira shook her head. "I didn't know you liked plants."

Colleen sighed. "I didn't know you did, either."

Chip stirred on his pillow, and Moira scooped him up and handed him to Colleen. "There is such a thing as a second chance, you know."

Colleen buried her nose in the puppy's soft fur and nodded. Second chances. Yes. She did know. Unfortunately, she wasn't quite so sure about thirds.

Colleen forged through the biting cold wind with her head down, taking the steps to the court building as quickly as possible. She wasn't looking forward to standing next to Ned Jones or facing Eric, but the damage had been done.

At the entrance to the courthouse, she reached for the door handle just as the door swung open. "Excuse me," she murmured at the feet standing in front of her. "I—"

"Colleen."

Her gaze shot to his face and she froze. God, he

looked beautiful. Distant, but beautiful. "Eric." She swallowed. "What are you—"

"We settled the Esther Wellington case today. The contractor buckled under pressure."

She forced a tight smile. "That's wonderful. Congratulations."

He nodded once, lips pressed together.

"So—" she cleared her throat "—Chip's officially my mom's dog. No chip in Chip."

"That's great," Eric said. Remote. Self-protective. "He seemed to make your mom happy."

Silence.

Awkward.

Their gazes met and bounced off each other.

"Well," he said finally, "see you in there."

"Yes. Okay."

He skirted around her without another word and strode down the vast steps, the vent flap of his overcoat blowing in the unforgiving wind.

Colleen stood shivering at the top of the courthouse steps and watched him walk away. Again. Why was she always watching him walk away?

Go time.

The courtroom was familiar, smelling of lemon wood polish, old leather and men's cologne. She somehow felt completely different. Off her game.

She'd lined up her notes like usual. Positioned her water glass like usual. Warned her client not to say a word unless instructed by her, like usual. Still, something about this hearing felt very, very unusual. She was in the midst of wracking her brain to figure it out just as the bailiff called, "All rise!" to the courtroom. The shuffle of feet and chair legs sounded the collective response to that oh-so-familiar order.

She straightened her suit jacket.

Didn't look at Eric. He stood just across the center aisle from her, but it felt as if he were on another continent. And she without a passport. Story of her life.

The balding judge entered in a swirl of black fabric. "Have a seat, people. Let's get this show on the road."

As they sat, the judge began his instructions, which she sort of listened to, sort of blew off. She practically had them committed to memory. Just before they were to begin opening arguments, her cell phone trilled. Damn it! She always remembered to turn it off. The judge turned a steely eye her way. Flustered—and she was *never* flustered in the courtroom—Colleen wrangled her phone out of her purse and randomly pushed buttons with fingers that felt linebacker huge. The damn thing seemed to get louder, although she knew that was due to embarrassment only.

She hit a button and the photo of her and Eric appeared on her screen. She gasped, couldn't look away. A million pairs of eyes aimed her way, and still she couldn't look away from that photo of perfection. The truth of the matter struck her. She'd fought so hard to avoid having a life like her mother's, twisting herself into knots for a man, and she'd turned out like her. Only not in the man-hunting way. She'd exchanged man-hunting for career achievement above all else, and in doing so had made a grave error in judgment.

"Counselor?" the judge boomed.

Nothing.

"Colleen," Eric rasped from across the aisle.

"What's wrong?" Ned Jones whispered.

"Ms. Delaney," began the judge, clearly annoyed. "Could you please approach—"

Her gaze shot up. "Your honor, I need…I need to leave."

He pulled his chin back and frowned. "Excuse me?"

"I have an emergency."

Judge Moher sighed hugely. "How long do you need?"

"I don't know."

"Very well. This court is adjourned until tomorrow morning same time. And there better not be a single cell phone on in my courtroom tomorrow."

Crack! went the gavel.

Ned peppered her with questions, but she fended

him off, gathering her things with shaky hands. Eric and his clients sat with heads together as she rushed from the courtroom. She needed space to figure this out. Time. Memories.

Harrison Scott, apparently, had been sent to watchdog her from the back of the courtroom. The fact that she hadn't noticed him spoke volumes about her attention level.

He caught up with her on the steps. "Colleen."

She spun to face him. The wind whipped both of their coats to the side, chapped her skin.

"What in the hell happened in there?"

"I can't do it."

His eyes narrowed. "What?" he spat.

"I can't do it, Harrison. I can't sell out for the firm. Not anymore. There are more important things in life than a partnership." She handed over the files.

"You're making a huge mistake."

"I already made one." She shook strands of her hair away from her face. "Do what you want with Ned Jones. My resignation will be on your desks by five this afternoon." And with that, she left him slackjawed. Skipping down the steps, she felt lighter than she had in years.

Eric left the courtroom baffled. He didn't want to feel anything for Colleen, but it had moved far beyond that option with him. He hoped her mother was okay. The urge to call her waged a strong war inside him, but he fought it off. He'd just arrived at his office and loosened his tie when his own cell phone bleeped. Incoming text. And photo?

From Colleen?

His heart lifted, in spite of himself. He clicked on the text:

Dear Santa—
I realize it's early, but I wanted to get in ahead of the holiday rush. See, I'm unemployed, which is okay, but I've screwed up and hurt someone I love. All I want for Christmas is this. (Click photo)

Unemployed? Colleen was unemployed? Since when?

Eric opened the picture of him kissing Colleen, and his legs weakened. He sank into his desk chair and stared at the photo. She looked so incredible. They looked so happy, so meant for each other.

Another text message intruded.

He hated to click away from the photo, but he did it anyway. It read:

Interested? Curious? You know where to find me, Sugar Baby.

The conservatory.

Eric didn't even bother to fix his tie. Standing, he threw on his coat and burst out of his office.

Jennifer jumped. "Geez, you scared me. Are you okay?"

"I'm fantastic. I'm going to be gone the rest of the day, though."

She blinked in confusion. "Should I—"

He spun to face her as he walked backward toward the elevators. "Reschedule all my appointments, Jen. You're getting a raise, by the way."

"Okay…thank you."

He lifted his hand in a wave and jogged the rest of the way to the elevators. Maybe, for Colleen and him, the third time would be the charm.

Colleen finally knew what it meant to just be.

She sat on the bench at the conservatory, right next to the Rumrilla Sugar Baby, and knew that whatever happened was supposed to happen. Until then, she closed her eyes and listened to the beautifully deafening quiet of the gardens. She inhaled the rich scents. She felt fully present in the moment and at peace.

Before long, someone sat next to her on the bench. She smiled, opened her eyes.

He searched her face. "Shouldn't you have a cup by your side?"

"What?"

"For coins. I heard you're unemployed."

"I am. Thank God."

"What happened?"

"I came to my senses. I couldn't defend Ned Jones. You were right, it was just a stupid case. I'd been so focused, I lost sight of the fact that I have a choice in this life. And I couldn't stomach working for that bunch one moment longer. Most of all, I couldn't bear the look of hurt and disgust in your eyes." She edged closer to him and reached for his hand. "Eric, I'm sorry. Everything closed in on me and I—"

"Ran scared."

"Yes."

"Again."

"I know. Does it help if I tell you I'll never do it again?"

He draped his arm around her waist, and she rested her head on his shoulder. "What kind of assurances can you give?"

"Well, the Gold Coast doesn't come cheaply. Forgive me for being forward, but I've hung back far too long. Are you interested in some roommates for that big house of yours?"

"Nope."

Her breathing hitched before she could remind herself to "just be."

"But I am interested in family."

She swallowed thickly. "You mean, Brian and the others?"

"No." He smoothed his hand down her cheek, kissed her gently on the lips. "I mean a wife. Kids. Even a mother-in-law in the carriage house."

"And her little dog, too?" she teased, although love clogged Colleen's chest.

"Absolutely. A chicken in every pot, a dog in every yard."

"Eric?"

"Yes?"

"Are you asking me to marry you?"

"Yes. Are you accepting?"

"Nothing would make me happier. Although a new job would be the icing on the wedding cake."

"I can probably help you out there, too. You can work at our firm. Fast track to partnership, no Framus, no McTierney."

"And you know this because…?"

"I've been checking into things."

She cupped his face with both hands and kissed him deeply. "I was foolish to ever let you go."

"No kidding." He winked, then his expression sobered. "I have never loved another woman like I love you, Colleen, and I'll never try to change you. I love *you*."

She groaned. "God, I was such an idiot."

"Oh." He snapped his fingers. "I'll probably never let you forget that either. Sorry."

"You've earned the right." She glanced around them. "Can we be married here? And can the reception be catered by the Bourgeois Pig Cafe?"

"Anything you want."

"Well, then, Counselor, I'd say this case is closed."

Epilogue

The wedding had been simple, small, perfect. Colleen carried a bouquet of white roses—with thorns as a reminder—mixed in with Rumrilla Sugar Baby Orchids. Chip, who'd turned out to be the perfect little dog, wore a pillow on his back and served as the ring bearer.

When the "I dos" and "you may kiss the bride" parts were over, Colleen stood glowing next to her husband in the receiving line, hugging the guests and accepting their congratulations.

Jack Hanson and his wife, Samantha, approached.

He and Eric shook hands and did the obligatory back clap. "Thanks for clearing the case, pal."

"My pleasure. Glad the drama's over."

"Right." Jack pulled a droll face. "Kimi's home, dropped out of college like she'd threatened. The drama remains, the focus has just shifted."

Colleen peered up at her husband with curiosity.

"I'll explain it all later," he said, kissing her forehead.

Jack grinned at Colleen. "Glad we pulled you back from the dark side, doll. You look beautiful."

"Thank you. For the record, I'm glad Eric exonerated you and Robby Axelrod, too. It was the right thing to do."

Jack looked at Eric and aimed his thumb at Colleen. "Didn't I tell you, Nelson? Everything happens for a reason. And this woman happens to be a damn good reason."

Colleen laughed, head thrown back, bubbling with joy. She'd been doing a lot more of that lately.

The line dwindled, and Eric turned Colleen toward him. "I'm going to make you the happiest woman in the world."

She kissed him. "You already have." She tipped her bouquet toward him. "Just be prepared. I come with thorns."

"Ah, Coll. Haven't you figured it out yet? That's the reason I fell for you in the first place."

She raised her eyebrows. "Makes me wonder about your sanity, Nelson, I have to say."

He scoffed. "This coming from the woman who worked for Framus and Friends for—how many years was it?"

"Yeah, yeah. Point taken."

"Should we go mingle with our family?"

Family. A whole slew of them. And—God willing—more to come. Colleen tucked her hand in the crook of his arm and beamed up at him. "I'd love nothing more."

As they walked toward the throng of people who loved them, Colleen knew she'd never have to wish for another thing. She'd received her lifelong perfect gift.

A family of her very own.

* * * * *

*Don't miss the exciting conclusion
to the Special Edition continuity*
BACK IN BUSINESS

Kimiko Taka has always wanted her CEO
father to take her seriously. And now he has—
she's been given a job working for The Taka
Kyoto. But her straight-as-an-arrow hotel
manager Greg Sherman thinks Kimi is just a
rich playgirl looking for fun and games. What
will happen when the heiress and her boss
meet under the mistletoe?

Find out in
THE BOSS'S CHRISTMAS PROPOSAL
by Allison Leigh.
On sale December 2008,
wherever Silhouette Books are sold.

Here is a sneak preview of
A STONE CREEK CHRISTMAS,
the latest in Linda Lael Miller's acclaimed
MCKETTRICK *series.*

A lonely horse brought vet Olivia O'Ballivan
to Tanner Quinn's farm, but it's the rancher's
love that might cause her to stay.

A STONE CREEK CHRISTMAS.
Available December 2008
from Silhouette Special Edition.

Tanner heard the rig roll in around sunset. Smiling, he wandered to the window. Watched as Olivia O'Ballivan climbed out of her Suburban, flung one defiant glance toward the house and started for the barn, the golden retriever trotting along behind her.

Taking his coat and hat down from the peg next to the back door, he put them on and went outside. He was used to being alone, even liked it, but keeping company with Doc O'Ballivan, bristly though she sometimes was, would provide a welcome diversion.

He gave her time to reach the horse Butterpie's stall, then walked into the barn.

The golden retriever came to greet him, all wagging tail and melting brown eyes, and he bent to stroke her soft, sturdy back. "Hey, there, dog," he said.

Sure enough, Olivia was in the stall, brushing Butterpie down and talking to her in a soft, soothing voice that touched something private inside Tanner and made him want to turn on one heel and beat it back to the house.

He'd be damned if he'd do it, though.

This was *his* ranch, *his* barn. Well-intentioned as she was, *Olivia* was the trespasser here, not him.

"She's still very upset," Olivia told him, without turning to look at him or slowing down with the brush.

Shiloh, always an easy horse to get along with, stood contentedly in his own stall, munching away on the feed Tanner had given him earlier. Butterpie, he noted, hadn't touched her supper as far as he could tell.

"Do you know anything at all about horses, Mr. Quinn?" Olivia asked.

He leaned against the stall door, the way he had the day before, and grinned. He'd practically been raised on horseback; he and Tessa had grown up on their grandmother's farm in the Texas hill country, after their folks divorced and went their separate ways, both of them too busy to bother with a couple of kids. "A few things," he said. "And I mean to call you Olivia, so you might as well return the favor and address me by my first name."

He watched as she took that in, dealt with it, decided on an approach. He'd have to wait and see what that turned out to be, but he didn't mind. It was a pleasure just watching Olivia O'Ballivan grooming a horse.

"All right, *Tanner,*" she said. "This barn is a disgrace. When are you going to have the roof fixed? If it snows again, the hay will get wet and probably mold…"

He chuckled, shifted a little. He'd have a crew out there the following Monday morning to replace the roof and shore up the walls—he'd made the arrangements over a week before—but he felt no particular compunction to explain that. He was enjoying her ire too much; it made her color rise and her hair fly when she turned her head, and the faster breathing made her perfect breasts go up and down in an enticing rhythm. "What makes you so sure I'm a greenhorn?" he asked mildly, still leaning on the gate.

At last she looked straight at him, but she didn't

move from Butterpie's side. "Your hat, your boots—that fancy red truck you drive. I'll bet it's customized."

Tanner grinned. Adjusted his hat. "Are you telling me real cowboys don't drive red trucks?"

"There are lots of trucks around here," she said. "Some of them are red, and some of them are new. And *all* of them are splattered with mud or manure or both."

"Maybe I ought to put in a car wash, then," he teased. "Sounds like there's a market for one. Might be a good investment."

She softened, though not significantly, and spared him a cautious half smile, full of questions she probably wouldn't ask. "There's a good car wash in Indian Rock," she informed him. "People go there. It's only forty miles."

"Oh," he said with just a hint of mockery. "*Only* forty miles. Well, then. Guess I'd better dirty up my truck if I want to be taken seriously in these here parts. Scuff up my boots a bit, too, and maybe stomp on my hat a couple of times."

Her cheeks went a fetching shade of pink. "You are twisting what I said," she told him, brushing Butterpie again, her touch gentle but sure. "I meant…"

Tanner envied that little horse. Wished he had a furry hide, so he'd need brushing, too.

"You *meant* that I'm not a real cowboy," he said. "And you could be right. I've spent a lot of time on construction sites over the past few years, or in meetings where a hat and boots wouldn't be appropriate. Instead of digging out my old gear, once I decided to take this job, I just bought new."

"I bet you don't even *have* any old gear," she challenged, but she was smiling, albeit cautiously, as though she might withdraw into a disapproving frown at any second.

He took off his hat, extended it to her. "Here," he teased. "Rub that around in the muck until it suits you."

She laughed, and the sound—well, it caused a powerful and wholly unexpected shift inside him. Scared the hell out of him and, paradoxically, made him yearn to hear it again.

* * * * *

Discover how this rugged rancher's
wanderlust is tamed
in time for a merry Christmas, in
A STONE CREEK CHRISTMAS.
In stores December 2008.

Silhouette®

SPECIAL EDITION™

FROM *NEW YORK TIMES* BESTSELLING AUTHOR

LINDA LAEL MILLER

A STONE CREEK CHRISTMAS

Veterinarian Olivia O'Ballivan finds the animals in Stone Creek playing Cupid between her and Tanner Quinn. Even Tanner's daughter, Sophie, is eager to play matchmaker. With everyone conspiring against them and the holiday season fast approaching, Tanner and Olivia may just get everything they want for Christmas after all!

Available December 2008
wherever books are sold.

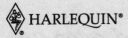

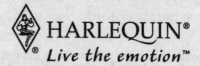

REQUEST YOUR FREE BOOKS!

2 FREE NOVELS PLUS 2 FREE GIFTS!

SPECIAL EDITION®

Life, Love and Family!

YES! Please send me 2 FREE Silhouette Special Edition® novels and my 2 FREE gifts (gifts are worth about $10). After receiving them, if I don't wish to receive any more books, I can return the shipping statement marked "cancel." If I don't cancel, I will receive 6 brand-new novels every month and be billed just $4.24 per book in the U.S. or $4.99 per book in Canada, plus 25¢ shipping and handling per book and applicable taxes, if any*. That's a savings of at least 15% off the cover price! I understand that accepting the 2 free books and gifts places me under no obligation to buy anything. I can always return a shipment and cancel at any time. Even if I never buy another book from Silhouette, the two free books and gifts are mine to keep forever.

235 SDN EEYU   335 SDN EEY6

Name	(PLEASE PRINT)	
Address		Apt. #
City	State/Prov.	Zip/Postal Code

Signature (if under 18, a parent or guardian must sign)

Mail to the Silhouette Reader Service:
IN U.S.A.: P.O. Box 1867, Buffalo, NY 14240-1867
IN CANADA: P.O. Box 609, Fort Erie, Ontario L2A 5X3

Not valid to current subscribers of Silhouette Special Edition books.

Want to try two free books from another line?
Call 1-800-873-8635 or visit www.morefreebooks.com.

* Terms and prices subject to change without notice. N.Y. residents add applicable sales tax. Canadian residents will be charged applicable provincial taxes and GST. Offer not valid in Quebec. This offer is limited to one order per household. All orders subject to approval. Credit or debit balances in a customer's account(s) may be offset by any other outstanding balance owed by or to the customer. Please allow 4 to 6 weeks for delivery. Offer available while quantities last.

Your Privacy: Silhouette is committed to protecting your privacy. Our Privacy Policy is available online at www.eHarlequin.com or upon request from the Reader Service. From time to time we make our lists of customers available to reputable third parties who may have a product or service of interest to you. If you would prefer we not share your name and address, please check here. ☐

SSE08R

Silhouette®

COMING NEXT MONTH

SSECNM1208BPA